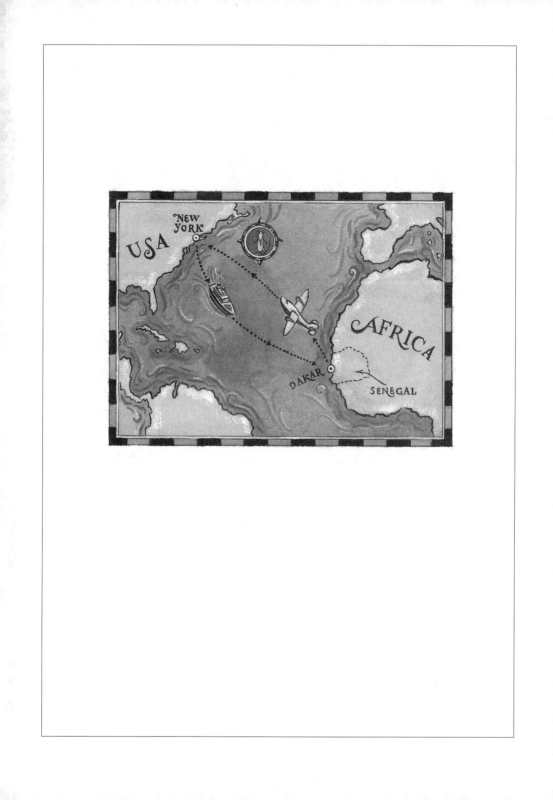

THE
REVENGE
OF
RANDAL
REESE-RAT

——— TOR SEIDLER ———

Pictures by
BRETT HELQUIST

FARRAR STRAUS GIROUX • NEW YORK

For Alexandra Collier and Jeannie Falls

Library of Congress Cataloging-in-Publication Data
Seidler, Tor.
    The revenge of Randal Reese-Rat / Tor Seidler ; pictures by Brett Helquist.— 1st ed.
        p. cm.
    Sequel to: A rat's tale.
    Summary: Musical Maggie Mad-Rat leaves her home in Africa to attend
her cousin Montague's wedding in New York City, where she meets family
and makes new friends, including the unique Randal Reese-Rat.
    ISBN 0-374-36257-2
    [1. Rats—Fiction. 2. Travel—Fiction. 3. Weddings—Fiction. 4. City and
town life—Fiction. 5. New York (N.Y.)—Fiction.] I. Helquist, Brett, ill.
II. Title.

PZ7.S45526 Re 2001
[Fic]—dc21

                                                                    2001016038

THE REVENGE OF RANDAL REESE-RAT

Elizabeth Mad-Rat loved warm, tropical places, but the midday African sun was more than she could take. It might have been bearable if she could have stopped to rest in the shade of one of the strange-looking African trees along the roadside, but she had no time to spare. The ship she'd come on, the SS *Ratterdam*, was leaving early the next morning to sail back to New York, and she was determined that she and her daughter should be on it.

The sun was so powerful that Elizabeth finally lifted her traveling case up over her head as a parasol. She'd found the suitcase, a French cigarette box with a dancing gypsy on it, years ago on the island of Martinique. It wasn't heavy—there was nothing in it but her comb and a seashell she'd picked up on a strip of beach on her way out of Dakar that morning—but her arms soon grew tired anyway.

3

I'm not as young a rat as I once was, she thought wistfully.

She finally stopped in the shade of a palm tree and collapsed on her traveling case. Once she had caught her breath, she realized how parched she was, and, seeing a thick vine twisted around the tree trunk like a spiral staircase, she started up it in search of a coconut. Last year, in Jamaica, she'd sipped some lovely milk from a broken coconut. But when she reached the top of the tree, there wasn't a coconut to be seen. Worse, even from way up there she couldn't make out the hill her daughter lived on.

"This is terrible," she muttered, realizing she must have taken a wrong turn on her way out of Dakar. "I'm a total nincompoop."

"Is that what you are?" said a squawky voice. "I wasn't sure. I thought maybe you were a rat."

If Elizabeth hadn't grabbed on with her tail at the last second, she would have tumbled out of the tree. Perched only two or three rat lengths away, camouflaged by the green palm fronds, was an enormous green bird with a vicious-looking hooked bill.

"Are total nincompoops native to Senegal?" the bird asked.

"I—I am a rat," Elizabeth said shakily. "But I'm not nearly as y-young and tasty as I once was."

The bird was bigger than a hawk, and for hawks rats were take-out food. But although the hooked bill looked capable of snipping her head off, the bird

just blinked at Elizabeth and said: "Senegalese rat?"

"No, I'm from . . . well, I'm not r-really from any-where. I travel a lot. But originally I'm from New York."

"New *York*. Is that near New Machavie?"

"Where's New Machavie?"

"In the south. I met a marabou from there once."

"The south of Africa?" said Elizabeth, who had no clue what a marabou was.

"Of course."

"No, New York's in the United S-States."

"Oooo, that sounds juicy! Nothing I like better than a snake breakfast."

"No, not United Snakes, United *States*."

"Oh." The bird looked disappointed. "I don't suppose states are as juicy."

"I have no idea, they're something to do with human beings." Elizabeth cleared her throat. "So you like to eat snake, but not rat?"

"No, I'm wild about rat. Especially for lunch."

Elizabeth shot a panicky look up through the fronds. Judging by the sun, it was between two and three o'clock, which was late for lunch in most places—but maybe not in Africa.

"It was l-lovely talking to you," she said, starting to back down the twisty vine.

"Why are you shivering, rat?"

"Am I shivering? I must be ch-chilly."

"But it's a hundred and one degrees Fahrenheit. Thirty-eight degrees Celsius." The bird cocked his head to one side. "I hope you're not thinking I'd eat you."

"But you said . . ."

"I like the taste of rat, but I wouldn't dream of eating one."

"You can't digest them?" Elizabeth said, stopping her descent.

"No, I can digest anything," the bird said, giving his feathers a quick preen. "My digestive system is as highly developed as my sense of temperature. I gave up rat out of respect for Maggie."

"Maggie? Not Maggie Mad-Rat?"

"That's the one."

Again Elizabeth nearly tumbled out of the tree—this time from surprise. "You know Maggie?"

"Everyone does."

"But she's my daughter!"

"Is she really? You must be very proud."

"Well, yes," Elizabeth said uncertainly.

"She's one of a kind, our Maggie."

Elizabeth wondered what this meant—for the sad truth was, she knew very little about her daughter. She'd given birth to her onboard the same New York–Dakar ship she'd disembarked from that morning, after which she'd spent a month in Dakar nursing the little ratling. This had been very hard on her—she hadn't spent that long in one place in ages—and as soon as Maggie was old enough to travel, they'd caught a ship to Belém, Brazil. But when Elizabeth had gotten ready to move on to Trinidad and Tobago, she'd learned that her daughter wasn't as mad for trekking to exotic, far-away places as she was.

"I'd like to go home, Mother," Maggie had said.

"Home?"

"Africa."

"But Africa's not your home, sweetie. It's just the first place you happened to put to shore, that's all."

"It's home to me. I love the open spaces, and the strong smells, and the animals—everything."

In the end they caught a ship back to Senegal. They found a nice spot for a nest outside Dakar, under the stump of a lightning-struck bakawana tree on top of a

7

hill that was shaped like a giant sleeping rat. But once Elizabeth had helped Maggie settle in, she couldn't hide her restlessness, and Maggie soon sent her on her way, assuring her that she could take care of herself. In the years since, Elizabeth had often meant to drop by for a visit—after all, Maggie *was* her only child—but the temptation to go somewhere new and different had always won out.

So she had no idea what the bird meant by "one of a kind." Maybe it was simply that Maggie was a New York City wharf rat by blood—no doubt a rare sub-species in West Africa.

"She's something all right," Elizabeth said noncommittally.

"You can say that again!" said the bird. "What a gift!"

"Gift?"

"Her music."

So that was it. When Maggie was born—on the ship's poop deck—a harmonica was lying nearby, fallen from a sailor's pocket. It had seemed like a sign of some kind, so Elizabeth had kept it for her.

"Plays her harmonica, does she?"

"I'll say!" said the bird. "Sings, too."

Like father, like daughter, Elizabeth thought, for her late husband had been a singer of songs.

"In fact," the bird went on, "I believe she's doing a sunset service today."

"A sunset service?"

"Yes. It's been dry as a rhino's horn lately."

As if to illustrate this point, the palm fronds started to rustle dryly around them.

"I better catch this breeze," said the bird. "Maybe I'll see you at the service?"

"Could you tell me where it is?"

"Right on Maggie's hill."

"And which way exactly is that? I seem to have gotten my tail turned around."

"Just a few miles thataway," the bird said, inclining his head to the east. "Can't miss it. From a distance the hill looks exactly like a parrot sleeping with his head under his wing."

So saying, the bird opened his own impressive wings and flapped away. Elizabeth waited for the wind to die down before descending the vine, then she hoisted her traveling case over her head again and set out to the east. *Just a few miles*, she thought bitterly, trudging along. Easy for the bird to say, with those wings to glide on. *Dry as a rhino's horn*. Was it ever! She felt as if her fur was about to crackle and fall off. If only she would come across a nice swimming pool, like on one of her beloved cruise ships!

After a couple of hours she did come across some woods, where it was a little cooler. But as she emerged from under a big-leafed bush, she nearly bumped into a furry black creature with a long tail and a face almost as ugly as a human being's. The creature was far bigger than Elizabeth, but the stalk of a plant was sticking out of his mouth, meaning he was probably a vegetarian, not a rat-eater.

"Good afternoon," Elizabeth said, breathing through her mouth—for the beast didn't smell very good.

Instead of replying, the creature burst into hysterical laughter. Elizabeth, though no longer young, was still quite a beautiful rat, not used to being greeted with hysterical laughter. But then, she was too thirsty to stand on her dignity.

"Do you happen to know if there's any water in these woods, sir?"

The creature lifted his upper lip, exposing repulsive black gums, and laughed again.

"May I ask what's so funny?"

"I'm not a sir, I'm a monkey," he replied. "And it's not woods, it's jungle."

"Whatever it is, is there any water around?"

"Not lately."

If it really was a jungle, it wasn't a very big one, for

in less than an hour Elizabeth came out the other side onto a field of wispy brown grass. After passing underneath a barbed-wire fence, she got a whiff of something even worse than the monkey. And to think her daughter liked the smells of this place!

The reek came from a herd of bony cattle slurping at a water trough. The trough was far too high for a rat to drink from, but, fortunately for Elizabeth, cattle are as sloppy as they are smelly, and the beasts spilled more than enough onto the ground to quench her thirst.

Revived, she pattered along eastward, and as the sun sank behind her, she no longer had to carry her traveling case over her head. The sun was close to setting when she finally came in sight of Maggie's hill. It was just as she remembered: shaped like a sleeping rat, not a sleeping parrot.

But as she drew nearer, she was horrified to see— and hear—a major change since her last visit. They'd chosen the hill for its quiet seclusion, but now it was packed with noisy beasts, some furry, some feathery, some with horns, some with stripes, some smaller than Elizabeth, some bigger than taxicabs. Anxious as she was to reach her daughter, she couldn't possibly slip through this terrifying mob without being crushed or gobbled up.

"I see you made it, rat."

Elizabeth craned her neck and saw the big green bird perched directly overhead on the branch of a thorny bush.

"What's going on?" she asked. "Is this the sunset service?"

"Yes, it's about to start. Why don't you climb up here so you can see your daughter perform?"

Figuring it was too late for lunch anywhere, Elizabeth set down her traveling case and climbed the bush, carefully avoiding the thorns. As she found herself a perch, the host of raucous animals on the hillside fell silent.

"There she is," the bird whispered.

On a pulpit-like rock poking out above the mob, a pretty young she-rat appeared. At first Elizabeth thought she was holding fire in her paws—but it was the harmonica, catching the last ruddy rays of the sinking sun. The young she-rat lifted the instrument to her snout and started to play. Soon the entire congregation was swaying to her jazzy beat. Some of them—monkeys and chimpanzees, for the most part—clapped along, and certain birds began to whistle or chirp, and a nearby crocodile slapped his tail back and forth. But the instant the performer lowered the harmonica, everyone fell silent again.

The young she-rat began to sing. Her voice wasn't big, but it was miraculously clear and carried beautifully.

> *Up the river Senegal,*
> *Manantali Lake,*
> *Under sky without a cloud*
> *All day long it bake.*
>
> *Lake grow smaller every day.*
> *Then at night it shrink*
> *When all the thirsty animal*
> *Coming out to drink.*
>
> *Then the sun rise up again,*
> *Angry-faced and red,*

Making every animal
  Scurry off to bed.

But oh! at last the cloud come,
  Full of happiness
And rain that touch the waiting land
  Like a father's kiss.

After this, the singer lifted her harmonica again, and the whole audience sang the verses as she played. Just as they got to the last line, the sun dipped below the horizon. The young she-rat then backed off the rock, and after letting out a great cheer, the audience dispersed, heading off in all directions.

"That's it?" said Elizabeth.

"That's it," said the bird. "Let's hope it works."

So saying, the bird spread his great green wings and flew off into the ravishing African sunset.

Once the hillside was deserted, Elizabeth climbed down the thorny bush and lugged her traveling case up the slope. She found the young she-rat sitting on her harmonica near the bakawana stump, admiring the sunset.

"Hello, Maggie," Elizabeth said, setting down the cigarette box.

Turning, Maggie's pretty face registered surprise, then sheer amazement. "Mother?"

"Well, not much of one, I'm afraid, but the only one you've got. You've grown up, dear. You look marvelous."

Maggie rose slowly onto her hind legs. "Is it really you?"

"I must look like a dusty old wreck, but it is me."

"But you look beautiful!" Maggie rushed up and hugged her. "I can't believe you're here!"

Elizabeth laughed, tickling whiskers with her. "Look at you, my celebrity daughter. What a wonderful singing voice you have!"

"It comes from you, Mother. I still remember that song you used to sing:

> *Sailing, sailing*
> *Over the bounding main,*
> *Some rat'll skedaddle*
> *Clear to Seattle*
> *Ere you see me again."*

"Oh, I'm just a hack." Elizabeth took her daughter's paw in hers. "I'd forgotten you can see the ocean from up here, love."

"I always think of you when I look at it. But my goodness, Mother, you must be famished. Shall we have a bite out here and enjoy the sunset while we catch up?"

"That would be lovely."

Elizabeth picked up her traveling case and followed her daughter in under the stump. After freshening up in the guest room, she came back outside to find Maggie setting out a smorgasbord of strange-looking foods on a piece of colorful African cloth.

"I never have more than a little snack," said Elizabeth, who'd reached the age where she had to watch what she ate. "Where on earth did you get so many goodies?"

"The animals bring them to me as offerings. They think I'm a rainmaker."

"Are you, love?"

"I've been lucky a few times, that's all."

"Good gracious, what's this?" Elizabeth said, sniffing a yellowish lump.

"Water buffalo cheese from Ethiopia."

"And this?"

"It's an unfertilized flamingo egg from Tunisia."

"And this?"

"It's a rare fruit that grows on the banks of the river Nile. I forget the name."

"You've been to all these places?"

"Not all. But quite a few."

"Then you do like to travel," Elizabeth said, pleased.

"Actually, I'm still a homebody by nature. But they fly me around to places where they have bad droughts."

"Mon Dieu! How do you fly?"

"On different birds."

"And they never take a nip at you?"

"Not so far. But I want to hear about you, Mother. Tell me what you've been doing since I last saw you."

"Traveling, mostly," Elizabeth said, settling across from Maggie on the cloth. "Now what's this?"

"A nut. They grow lots of nuts here in Senegal. Try it."

Elizabeth took a nibble. It wasn't bad.

"Where have you traveled, Mother?"

"Let's see, I've taken cruises to the Bahamas, the Azores, Bermuda, the British Virgin Islands, the American Virgin Islands, Aruba, Barbados, the Yucatán Peninsula, the Mediterranean Sea, the Baltic—rather chilly up there—Rio de Janeiro, Grenada . . . Oh, and Hawaii. We went through the Panama Canal for that—quite an experience."

"Where did you just come from?"

"New York City. That's more or less my home base. I want you to come back there for a visit, Maggie. Our ship leaves at daybreak."

Maggie laughed. "But you just arrived, Mother. You can't be antsy already."

"We have a wedding to go to."

"A wedding!"

"Your cousin's."

"I have a cousin?"

Elizabeth sighed. "I really am the most miserable mother who ever lived. Not only did I desert you as soon as you were old enough to take care of yourself, I never gave you any family background."

"Do I have a family background?"

"Well, not much of an immediate family background. There's only me and . . ."

"You and who?"

"Well, dear, it's only me now, I'm afraid. Your father crossed the gulf into the land of dead rats."

The tips of Maggie's ears turned pale. "I'm sorry to hear that," she whispered. "Even if he was of no consequence."

Maggie had asked about her father when she was little, and that was how Elizabeth had described him.

"Did he die of thirst, Mother?"

"Hardly," Elizabeth said. "I'm afraid your father tippled."

"Tippled?"

"He liked his dandelion wine."

"You mean he was a drunken rat? Is that why he was of no consequence?"

Elizabeth squirmed a bit. "Your father wasn't of no consequence, Maggie. I told you that because . . . well, because otherwise you would have wanted to meet him, and I knew it would end up being a disappointment all around. He was no more cut out for being a father than I am for being a mother. All he cared about was doing up his rings."

Maggie looked over her shoulder at her mother's tail.

"What happened to your ring? I remember, it was so beautiful, with those suns and moons etched in the silver. Did my father make it?"

"Yes, he did. It was my wedding ring. I probably should have kept it for you, but I'm afraid I gave it away."

"That's all right, Mother. Rings are metal, and metal attracts heat. That's no good in Africa."

Off to the north, a huge half moon was rising. It made Elizabeth think of her late husband—Moony, he'd been called—and as she remembered the line about a father's kiss in Maggie's song, her eyes filled with tears. "Your father never knew about you, Maggie. I always assumed I'd tell him someday—but I kept traveling, and putting it off, and now—pffft!—he's gone. The only thing I can think to do is take you back so you can at least visit his grave. And meet your aunt and uncle and cousins."

"How did he die, Mother?"

"He got frozen."

"Frozen! It's that cold in New York?"

"It gets chilly in the winter, but this was August— just a couple of weeks ago. It's a long story, love. I'll tell you on the ship. We really better get going."

"Don't be silly, you just got here. You must be exhausted."

"I'll have a week onboard ship to catch up on my sleep. You see, I asked Monty to put off his wedding till we got back—and you know how impatient young rats are to get married, once they've proposed."

"Who's Monty?"

"Montague Mad-Rat. Your cousin—and your father's namesake. I'll fill you in on everything once we've set sail."

"But I can't go, Mother."

"What do you mean? Don't you want to broaden your horizons?"

"It's not that. It just hasn't rained in so long. They may want another sunset service tomorrow."

"But, love, you said it's all nonsense."

"Still, they count on me. I can't leave them in the lurch."

There was a firmness in Maggie's tone that told Elizabeth it wasn't going to be easy to change her mind. But the ship was leaving in less than twelve hours, and it would take several hours to get back to Dakar, so she did her best, describing the wonders of New York City: the skyline, the subways, the delicatessens full of cheese.

"It really is the rat center of the world, dear."

"It sounds marvelous, Mother. But I can't just take off."

"But you'll be treated like royalty, dear. It used to be other wharf rats looked down their snouts at us Mad-Rats, but that's all in the past."

"Why did they look down their snouts at us?"

"Oh, because we're a little unconventional. We don't

live on wharves and spend our time scouring the streets for money."

"Money? What's that?"

"Round bits of metal and pieces of paper."

"What's it for?"

"That's a good question, love. I had a hard time figuring it out. It's certainly not much use for building nests, and it tastes dreadful. But human beings are crazy about it—especially in the United States. Rats, too. That's why they like us now. You see, they have to pay rent to live on their wharves, but the human owner decided he could make more money turning them into parking lots. So he started poisoning the rats. But your father sold Monty's paintings to the art dealer he did his ring work for."

"Monty's a painter?"

"A very fine one. He paints on seashells I bring him from my travels. And they fetched such a price the wharf owner changed his mind. So Monty's a hero and everybody loves us Mad-Rats."

But not even the prospect of being treated like royalty could shake Maggie's sense of responsibility to her thirsty African friends. At last, utterly exhausted, Elizabeth dragged herself into the guest room.

After she'd been sleeping several hours, a vibration and a rumbling sound woke her up. For a moment she assumed she was in the Mad-Rats' sewer in New York and a subway was passing by. Then she remembered she was in Senegal, under the stump on Maggie's hill.

Lifting her head, she sniffed. Rats have a keen sense of smell, and Elizabeth detected something new in the dry night air. A distinct hint of moisture. Another rumble and she was up on her paws, scurrying to the entrance.

The moonlight had vanished. Rats have superb night vision, but Elizabeth couldn't even make out her own snout.

"Maggie?"

"Better stay inside, Mother."

In an instant night turned to noon. Everything was brilliantly clear: Maggie, standing with a grin on her snout just outside the nest; beyond her, a boulder shaped like a piece of Edam cheese; beyond that, a thorny bush; beyond that, the savanna stretching off to the glimmering sea.

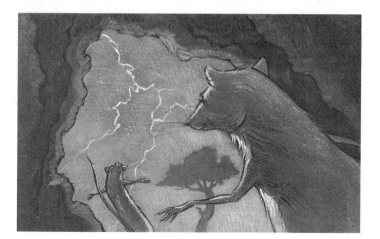

Then everything went black again. Another deep rumble vibrated through Elizabeth, all the way to the tip of her tail. A drumbeat of raindrops started up, and she felt her daughter's arm around her shoulders. Now the smell of moisture was more than just a hint. In seconds the temperature dropped fifteen degrees.

For an hour or more, mother and daughter stood side by side, safe and dry under the stump's overhang, staring out into a darkness now and then broken by lightning bolts that revealed a waterfall so close they could wash their paws in it. They didn't bother trying to speak. They could have screeched at the top of their lungs and the storm would have drowned them out.

Finally Nature quieted down. As the rain let up, a mouse-gray light seeped over the sky, and the waterfall turned into a trickle. The two rats ventured out onto the muddy hilltop. The clouds were being sucked off toward the sea. The wide plain below glistened wetly in the dawn.

"Will that do?" Elizabeth said.

Maggie beamed. "Lake Manantali will be swelling," she said.

"Then let's shake a paw. Maybe the storm will delay the ship."

Maggie didn't put up any more struggle. By the time Elizabeth came rushing out with her traveling case, her daughter was waiting for her with her harmonica tucked under one arm.

"Be careful, Mother, it's very—"

Elizabeth shrieked as her paws slipped out from under her on the slick slope. Maggie rushed to help her up.

"People!" Elizabeth cried. "I've twisted my hind foot. Now we'll never make it."

"Wait a second." Maggie walked over to a nearby hole in the ground. "Anybody home?" she called in.

To Elizabeth's horror, a cat—one of a rat's worst enemies—popped out. But unlike New York City alley cats, this one had spotted fur and a ringed tail, and though she showed her fangs, it was in a friendly smile.

"You did it again, Maggie!" the beast said.

"I doubt it was me," Maggie said modestly. "I hope your burrow's not flooded."

"A bit—but who cares? I haven't had such a good drink in weeks."

"Nagamba, this is my mother, Elizabeth. I was wondering if you'd give her a ride. She's twisted her foot and we have to get to the docks in Dakar as fast as possible."

"My pleasure," said Nagamba. "You might as well both hop on."

Appalled, Elizabeth motioned Maggie to her side. "I can't ride an alley cat," she whispered.

Maggie turned to Nagamba with a smile. "My mother's a foreigner. She thinks you're an alley cat."

"I'm a genet, madam," Nagamba said politely, "and a big fan of your daughter."

Elizabeth had no idea what a genet was, but Maggie

virtually shoved her up onto the creature's spotted back. She perched there nervously while Maggie climbed on behind her.

"Hold on tight," Nagamba cried.

As the genet bounded away, Elizabeth held on for dear life, eyes squeezed shut, jaw clenched. But after a while she cracked one eye. The countryside was a blur—yet the ride was as smooth as a cruise on calm seas.

"Isn't this fun?" Maggie said in her ear.

Amazingly enough, it was. They rode along with a cool, fresh wind in their faces, not having to exert themselves in the slightest, and not even getting wet, thanks to the genet's acrobatic knack for avoiding puddles. To Elizabeth's delight, they didn't even have to slow down when they entered the city of Dakar, since most of the human beings were still in bed. The genet sprinted alongside the running gutters and dodged agilely across intersections, once diving right between the wheels of a jeep.

At the waterfront there *was* human activity. Brutish men were loading and unloading ships; others were setting up stalls in a bazaar; others were sitting under canopies sipping from cups and smoking while women carried things around on their heads.

"See that big pile of fishnets?" cried Elizabeth. "The dock's just past that."

Their chauffeur whizzed them through a crowd of people, around the nets, and out onto the dock where

Elizabeth had landed yesterday. As soon as the genet stopped, Elizabeth jumped off. She landed right on her twisted hind foot, but the cry she let out wasn't on account of the pain. The SS *Ratterdam* was steaming toward the headland, on its way out to sea.

"That's the ship?" said Maggie, dismounting.

"Gone!" Elizabeth cried. "Left without us!"

"Well, there's bound to be another one to New York, Mother."

"But who knows when! Do you have any fishy friends who'd swim us out to the ship?"

"My only fishy friends are freshwater fish in the Senegal River and Lake Manantali, places like that. Even in droughts, the ocean never shrinks."

"Oh dear. I said two weeks—and now . . . Poor Monty!"

Montague Mad-Rat certainly wasn't feeling like "poor Monty" the last time he saw his aunt. In fact, he was in rat heaven. Not because his shell paintings had fetched a fortune and turned him from sewer rat to rat hero. That had been mostly his uncle's doing, and poor Uncle Moony had ended up dead for his troubles. No, the source of Montague's happiness was Isabel Moberly-Rat. Isabel had championed his paintings, too—and she was the most dazzling young she-rat he'd ever met, with beautiful beady gray eyes and radiant fur and a blue ribbon around her neck.

The last time Montague saw his aunt he'd just spent the night with Isabel in Central Park. He'd run into Isabel near the Great Lawn and they'd ended up sleeping on Uncle Moony's grave, under a laurel bush on the bank of the reservoir. In the morning Isabel woke first, feeling a strange warmth at the base of her tail. It was the morning sun, hitting a lovely silver ring that Montague's aunt, Elizabeth, had given her the day before on her wharf. Then Isabel felt a whir of guilty excitement. After helping take Montague's shell paintings to the art gallery, she'd spent an awful night stuck in a garbage can, but every other night of her life had been spent in her plush bedroom in crate 11 on Wharf 62— and here she was, curled up in Central Park beside Montague Mad-Rat!

Or was it just a dream? When they'd dozed off the night before, Montague hadn't had a ring on his tail— and now he was wearing one exactly like hers. She poked herself with the tip of her tail. But this didn't wake her up, so after a moment she poked Montague.

Montague blinked at her and grinned. "Morning, Izzy," he said, stretching.

"Morning, Monty."

"Sleep well?"

"Mm. But I don't think you did."

"Why do you say that?"

"Where'd you get that?"

Montague looked at his tail. "Good grief, my uncle's ring!"

"Where'd you find it?"

"I didn't." The last time Montague saw his uncle, the ring had been missing from his uncle's tail. "I figured Pembroke stole it."

"That wouldn't surprise me," said Isabel, who'd met Pembroke Pack-Rat, Uncle Moony's shifty-eyed business associate, on her art-gallery adventure.

"But that means Pem must have snuck up in the middle of the night and slipped it on my tail."

"That *would* surprise me," said Isabel. "But who knows, maybe even pack rats have consciences. He must have known your uncle would have wanted you to have it."

"Mm, it was his wedding ring."

The tips of Isabel's ears blushed. The matching rings were wedding rings!

"Gad," she said, brushing leaf bits off her fur. "I have to be getting home."

"Why?"

"Mother will be doing back flips."

This was unlikely, considering Mrs. Moberly-Rat's cheese-related weight problems, but Montague was thinking of his own mother. "What about my mom's supplies, Izzy?" he cried.

His mother spent her time making rat hats in the broken-down sewer pipe where the Mad-Rats lived. Montague had come to the park yesterday to collect feathers and berries for her, and last night Isabel had agreed to help him.

"But I should never have stayed out all night with you," she said.

"Why not?"

"It's not proper—for unmarried rats."

Having grown up in a sewer, Montague had never learned the finer points of wharf-rat etiquette, but this particular problem seemed easy enough to solve. "Don't you want to marry me, Izzy?" he said.

"Gad, Monty! Are you proposing?"

"Well, I guess I kind of assumed . . ."

"You assumed I'd want to marry you now that you're Montague the Magnificent, savior of ratkind?"

"No, no, I just meant . . . You're not in love with that Randal Reese-Rat, are you?"

Isabel's beautiful eyes widened. "How in the world do you know about Randal?"

"I saw you with him last week. His father's a big rat leader like yours, right?"

"Mm, Clarence Reese-Rat. Not *quite* as important as Daddy, but he's one of the ministers."

"And Randal lives on that same fancy wharf as you?"

"Mm, crate 8. We were sort of engaged."

Montague swallowed. "Do you still love him?"

Isabel gazed out at a pair of ducks—one with iridescent green neck feathers, the other with dull brown—floating together on the sun-dappled reservoir. As far back as she could remember, everybody had assumed that she and Randal Reese-Rat would become a couple. When the poisoning of the wharves started, Randal had gotten poison on his tail, and just before passing out, he'd finally proposed to her. She'd accepted joyfully, and after returning from her art-gallery adventure she'd rushed straight to his sickroom. But she'd been such a mess (this was just after the Night of the Garbage Can) that Randal, who was an extremely neat and tidy rat, had rejected her. Under normal circumstances, rejection increases a rat's eagerness, but since then Isabel had gotten to know Montague . . .

"I just thought," Montague said rather desperately, "when we twined tails last night . . ."

"You figured that meant we love each other?"

"Well . . ."

Isabel scooted over beside him, figuring she'd tortured him long enough. "Of course we do!" she said, twining her tail in his again.

"So we can get married?"

"I don't see why not."

"Hooray! Can we do it today?"

Isabel laughed her bright, tinkling laugh. Rats aren't patient creatures—their courtships rarely last more than a few hours—but then, she *was* a Moberly-Rat.

"It might be more proper to wait till tomorrow," she said. "Arrangements have to be made."

A whole day seemed an awfully long time to wait, but even so Montague was in rat heaven—till they finished collecting berries and feathers for his mother's hatmaking. Then he got nervous. Isabel had never seen his home before.

When he led her into his family's sewer pipe, he was relieved to see that it wasn't as smoky as usual. With no berries to melt down into dyes, his mother had let the fires go out under her dye vats. Nor were his neglected ratling brothers and sisters screeching as piercingly as usual, for Aunt Elizabeth was there to play with them.

"Monty, thank heavens!" Mrs. Mad-Rat cried, rushing up and grabbing the feathers from his tail. "When you didn't come yesterday, I was nearly suicidal—but look, double supplies!" She grabbed Isabel's feathers, too. "Who's your wonderful friend, dearie?"

Montague spat his berries into a vat. Once Isabel had done the same, he introduced her to his mother.

"So nice to meet you, Mrs. Mad-Rat," Isabel said. After shaking paws, she turned to Elizabeth, who was sitting on her cigarette box with a bunch of ratlings in her lap. "I just love the ring," she said.

"Good, because I never really deserved it," said Elizabeth. "Why, Monty, you've got Moony's!"

"Isn't it amazing?" said Montague. "Hey, Dad, there's someone I want you to meet!"

Mr. Mad-Rat spent his time building mud castles on the caved-in slope at the end of the sewer. He slapped mud off his paws as he weaved his way down off the slope.

"You built all those castles, Mr. Mad-Rat?" Isabel said. "There must be a hundred!"

"I'm on 108," Mr. Mad-Rat said. "I have a hunch it's going to be one of my best."

Montague cleared his throat importantly. "Mom, Dad, Aunt Elizabeth," he said. "Izzy and I want to get married."

"Good idea," said Mr. Mad-Rat, who'd taken an in-

stant liking to Isabel on the basis of her admiration for
his castles.

Mrs. Mad-Rat was already busy pawing through her
new feathers. "Does that mean I'll always be getting
double supplies?" she said, glancing hopefully over her
shoulder.

"When were you thinking of, Monty?" Aunt Elizabeth asked.

"Tomorrow."

"No use wasting time," said Mr. Mad-Rat, who felt
he was wasting time that should have been devoted to
castle 108.

"You know, Isabel," said Mrs. Mad-Rat, "if you like,
you could wear one of my hats at the wedding."

Here was an extraordinary offer. The curved walls of the sewer were hung with hundreds of feathered rat hats, but as a rule Mrs. Mad-Rat couldn't bear to part with any of them for an instant. And, indeed, she quickly had second thoughts. "Though, of course, there aren't any white ones. Is this your first marriage, dearie?"

"Of course it is!" Isabel cried.

"Well, in that case, I don't suppose you'd want a red or a purple hat. But then, it seems a pity to have a hatless wedding. Maybe *I* could wear one."

"Oh, do!" said Isabel. "They're remarkable."

"Why, thank you. I can tell you're going to make a lovely daughter-in-law. Now, tell me your last name again?"

"Moberly-Rat."

"Well, that's just grand."

"Don't worry," said Isabel, who was used to her name making an impression. "My father may be a bigwig, but he's not a bit scary once you get to know him."

"Your father, dear?" said Mrs. Mad-Rat.

"Wears a wig, does he?" said Mr. Mad-Rat, inching off toward his castles. "We won't hold that against him."

"Even if hats are preferable to wigs," Mrs. Mad-Rat murmured, turning back to her feathers.

"They don't know much about other rats, Izzy," Montague said in an undertone. "We're kind of out of the rat loop down here."

"Oh," said Isabel, deflated.

Mr. Mad-Rat climbed back up his muddy slope, and Mrs. Mad-Rat started lighting the fires under her vats. The ratlings tugged at Aunt Elizabeth, but she asked them to give her a minute.

"Monty," she said, "I have a favor to ask of you. It's about your wedding."

"You'll stay, won't you? You don't have to leave on a cruise this afternoon?"

"No, I don't *have* to leave this afternoon—though I am beginning to feel a bit cooped up down here."

"No horizons," Montague said sympathetically.

"You know me so well, dear," she said, smiling. "But there's one thing you don't know."

"What's that, Aunt Elizabeth?"

"Well, it's something Moony didn't even know. That he and I had a child. Your cousin."

"My cousin! What's his name?"

"Her name. Maggie. And that's why I want to ask if you'd postpone your wedding."

"We already are, Aunt. Till tomorrow."

"I was going to ask you to postpone it a little longer."

"Longer? How much longer?"

"Two weeks."

"Two weeks!" Montague cried in dismay. "But why?"

"Because that's how long it takes to sail to Africa and back."

Elizabeth described the scene in the sewer pipe to Maggie as they watched the SS *Ratterdam* round the headland on its way out of Dakar harbor.

"Poor Cousin Montague," Maggie said. "But surely they'll go ahead with the wedding without us."

"I made him promise to wait."

"And there won't be another ship for how long?"

"You never can tell. It might be a few days, it might be two or three weeks."

"Well, I'll tell you one rat who won't be on it, Mother."

"Who?"

"Me."

"But, Maggie, what do you mean?"

"They'll blame me for delaying things so long. Why should I go somewhere just to be resented?"

Aunt Elizabeth felt like crying. She'd gone to all this

trouble—crossing an ocean, trekking under the blazing African sun, waiting out a lightning storm, riding on the back of a cat—to fetch her daughter, but in her heart she knew Maggie was right. Montague and Isabel would be polite to her, of course, but they would resent her for keeping them apart so long. According to wharf-rat etiquette, rats can't snuggle up together till they're married.

The genet was clearly pleased by Maggie's decision not to leave. "If you'd caught that ship and come back in a month, that would be one thing," Nagamba said. "Last night's rain'll last us a month. But if you went in a week and didn't come back for another month after *that*, you might be gone when we need you."

Maggie agreed. "But don't be down in the snout, Mother. At least you can have a nice visit here. You'll feel better once you get some more sleep."

Maggie took her mother's paw to lead her off the dock, but Elizabeth wouldn't budge.

"Your foot still hurts?" Maggie said. "I'm sure we could get a ride."

"My pleasure," said the genet.

"I have an idea, Maggie," Elizabeth said. "You say birds fly you places. Couldn't you get one to fly us out to the ship?"

"I've only dealt with land birds, Mother. The ones who like to fly over the ocean are sea birds."

"But surely a land bird would take a little risk for *you*." Elizabeth squinted up at the sky. "There's one now! Wave him down, Maggie—before the ship gets too far away!"

Rats have very sharp eyes for things close up, but their long-distance vision leaves something to be desired. "I'm afraid that's not a bird, Mother of Maggie," said the genet. "It's one of those things human beings fly in."

"Oh, an airplane," said Elizabeth, disappointed. "But, Maggie, there must be a bird hereabouts who knows you. I met a big green one yesterday who thinks you're the rat's pajamas."

"I don't see any birds—except that pelican," Maggie said, nodding at a strange-looking bird perched on a sack of sorghum at the end of the dock. "He doesn't look familiar."

"Goodness, what a big bill!" Elizabeth said. "Maybe he'd give us a ride in it."

"I don't think you'd care for the smell, Mother. It's an acquired taste."

"Oh, I could stand anything for a few minutes."

Elizabeth limped over toward the bird. "Excuse me, Mr. Pelican," she said. "But I was wondering if you'd give me and my daughter a lift out to that ship in your bill."

"What ship is that?"

To speak the pelican naturally opened his bill, and the reek of rotten fish that came out of it knocked Elizabeth backward. In comparison, yesterday's monkey had smelled like a bowl of rose petals.

"You were right," Elizabeth confessed, trudging back to Maggie and the genet. She squinted skyward again. "Are you sure that one up there's just an airplane?"

"Positive," said the genet. "It looks as if it just took off from the . . . the place where they take off."

"The airport," said Elizabeth, who knew such things from her world travels. Suddenly she perked up. "Do you know where the airport is?"

"Just outside of town, Mother of Maggie."

"Why do you ask?" Maggie wondered.

"Well, love, I've always said that if rats were meant to fly, they'd have wings. But if *you* can fly on a bird, I suppose I could fly in an airplane." She peered up again. "They look as if they're faster than ships, too. Imagine if we arrive early—they'll welcome us with open arms! Will you run us to the airport, Nagamba?"

"Would that mean you'll be back sooner, Maggie?" the genet asked.

"I suppose," said Maggie.

"Then what are we waiting for!"

On their way back out of Dakar they had to proceed haltingly, stopping to hide in doorways and behind baskets, for the streets were growing crowded with people, and two rats riding along on the back of a genet was an unusual spectacle. But in a couple of hours the genet deposited her passengers safely in front of the main terminal at Dakar International Airport.

They thanked their chauffeur and bid her farewell, Maggie promising to be back before long. Maggie then

started to join the stream of people heading for the automatic doors, but Elizabeth stopped her, explaining that they would have to stow away in some luggage. So they scuttled around the side of the terminal to a baggage loading dock on the edge of the runway. The loading dock was piled high with suitcases, but although there were tags on all the handles, the rats couldn't decipher the destinations.

"We could just as easily end up in Bombay or Helsinki as New York," Elizabeth said with a sigh. "I've got to sit down to think. My foot hurts."

While Elizabeth rested on her cigarette box, Maggie set down her harmonica and continued poking around. She soon came upon a piece of luggage that yapped.

Putting an eye up to an airhole, she saw that there was a dog inside: a fancily clipped poodle.

"Where are you heading, poodle?" she asked.

"*A Paris, bien sûr,*" the poodle said.

A lot of French is spoken in West Africa, so Maggie understood that the dog was bound for Paris, France. Near the poodle was a cage containing a monkey who claimed to be bound for the Rome Zoo. Beyond his cage was a bigger one with a warthog in it.

"Where are you going, warthog?" Maggie asked.

"A place called the Bronx Zoo," the warthog said mournfully.

The only other cage contained a sleeping python, and not even Maggie dared strike up a conversation with a python, so she returned to her mother, discouraged.

"I found some animals, but none heading for New York."

"Where are they going, dear?"

"Paris, Rome, and a place called the Bronx."

"But the Bronx is part of New York!"

"Really?"

"Absolutely! Very popular with rats."

Elizabeth followed her daughter over to the Bronx-bound cage—and was knocked backward again. Not by the warthog's bad breath but by his ugliness. In all her travels she'd never laid eyes on such a hideous creature.

But Maggie assured her in an undertone that warthogs weren't rat-eaters, and when Maggie asked the creature if he'd mind company on his journey, he was overjoyed. So after Maggie squeezed into the cage, Elizabeth followed suit—though she kept her distance from the warthog's snout, with its bizarre bumps and horns.

Just as she was settling comfortably into the wood chips that lined the bottom of the cage, the cage jolted to life. A conveyor belt loaded it onto a cart that rolled across a sunny runway into the shadow of a jet plane. A pair of human beings with turbans on their heads set the cage into the plane's hold along with some wooden crates and then shut them in.

The hold was hot and stuffy.

"It's going to be a long week," Elizabeth sighed, peering out at the cramped quarters. "No portholes, no deck chairs, no swimming pool. Not even shuffle-board."

Before long, the airplane jiggled and jerked forward. Then it stopped. Then it began to shudder, as if it might fall to pieces. Then it heaved forward again, slowly at first, then faster and faster, till Elizabeth had to grab a bar of the cage with a paw to keep from slid-ing between the warthog's hooves.

Once the plane steadied into an easy climb, the tem-perature in the hold started to drop. Soon it was quite pleasant, and the warthog settled back on his haunches and grinned at his two fellow passengers.

"Do you rats like riddles?" he asked hopefully.

"Sure," said Maggie.

The warthog's grin widened, showing a mouthful of very bad teeth. "Ready?"

"All set," said Maggie.

"Okay. Why didn't the monkey want to play games with the jungle cat?"

"Why?" said Maggie.

"It was a cheetah!"

The warthog snorted hilariously.

"Not bad," Maggie said.

"Okay, here's another. Ready?"

"Ready."

"What kind of fruit do giraffes like best?"

"Let me think," said Maggie. "Bananas?"

"No, neck-tarines." Snort, snort. "Get it? Giraffes—*neck*-tarines."

"I get it," said Maggie.

"Okay. Ready for another?"

"Ready," said Maggie.

"You ready?" the warthog asked, eyeing Elizabeth.

"Ready," Elizabeth said, covering a yawn.

"Okay. Why don't leopards like to play hide 'n' seek?"

"Because they're always spotted?" Maggie guessed.

The warthog looked as if he'd just been shot. "You've heard it," he groaned.

"Mm, in Ghana."

The warthog screwed up his face in concentration, then smiled his toothy grin again. "Okay, here's one I bet you don't know! Why do lions eat raw meat?"

Now Maggie yawned. It wasn't that she was bored, it

was just that the hold was growing chillier and chillier, and cold makes rats sleepy. "Why?" she asked.

"Because they don't know how to cook!" Snort, snort, snort.

As the warthog rattled off more riddles, it got colder and colder, and Elizabeth, who was exhausted anyway, fell fast asleep. Soon Maggie did, too.

"Rats," the warthog muttered, miffed. "No sense of humor."

But it wasn't long before he, too, dozed off, and all three of them remained dead to the world till a violent jolt woke them up. There was a skidding sound, followed by a deafening whoooosh. Gradually the plane slowed down.

"I believe we're back on the ground," said the warthog.

"But where?" Elizabeth wondered.

"New York City?" Maggie guessed.

"Impossible, dear. There's a whole ocean to cross."

But to Elizabeth's wonder and surprise, the odor that drifted into the hold when the hatch opened was unmistakably New York City: a subtle mixture of exhaust fumes, damp pavement, human body odor, and hot pretzels.

"Good grief, we're here!" she exclaimed. "Look, the sun's still out. We leave in the morning and arrive the same afternoon! It's a miracle!"

"We gained hours," said the warthog.

"How do you gain hours?" Maggie asked.

"That's a riddle I don't have the answer to. I just heard some human beings talking about it."

"Speak of the devil," said Elizabeth, burrowing under the wood chips as a pair of gigantic human beings in coveralls opened the door to the hold and clambered in.

Maggie hid, too. The giants loaded the warthog's cage onto a hydraulic lift, and from the lift into the back of a van. The giants got in, too, and sat by the cage as the van rolled away.

"Jeez, look at this guy," said one of them.

"And I thought my mother-in-law has an ugly mug," said the other.

They should talk, thought Elizabeth, peering through

the wood chips at the monstrous, furless beasts. Still, if she and Maggie could get a ride partway to the Mad-Rats', she supposed she could stand to share the back of the van with them.

But the van stopped after traveling only a short distance. The back door was thrown open by a human being wearing glasses and a white coat.

"Inspection!" he cried. "Can't have any African parasites coming into the good old U.S. of A.!"

Elizabeth had no idea what a parasite was, but she didn't like the sound of "Inspection" one bit.

"We better scat," she whispered, poking Maggie with her tail, and as the giants lifted the cage out of the van, she hastily thanked the hospitable warthog for his riddles and jumped out.

Elizabeth swallowed her "Ouch" as she hit the pavement, and the second that Maggie landed beside her, she dragged her behind one of the van's tires. From there they scampered around the side of the airline terminal to a long line of idling yellow cabs and crouched underneath the one in front while the cabby helped his passenger put his suitcases in the trunk. Once the trunk closed and the human beings climbed into the cab, the rats hopped up on the back bumper. Soon they were moving along even faster than on the genet. It was a bouncy ride, and there were countless cars and cabs in their wake, so Maggie clutched her harmonica under her arm and gripped the bumper with her tail to keep from being thrown under the oncoming tires.

Only when the cab slowed down did Maggie have a chance to peer left and right. They were in the middle of an enormous city, sailing through a sea of buildings. After a moment the taxi came to a halt. Then the cabby honked his horn, and they magically sped up.

This became a pattern. Slowing to a crawl, the magical honking, speeding up again. After about an hour of this, they crossed a magnificent bridge.

"Welcome to Manhattan Island, dear," Elizabeth said.

"You mean we're leaving New York City?"

"No, Manhattan's part of the city."

Soon the taxi came to a dead stop. The cabby laid on his horn again; so did the drivers behind them. But the magic didn't seem to work in Manhattan. They were stuck. Between the honking and the fumes from the exhaust pipe, the two rats got such splitting headaches that they had to jump off the bumper and proceed on foot.

In the end, the fifteen miles from the airport to the Mad-Rats' sewer pipe seemed to take longer than the five thousand miles from Africa to New York. Elizabeth limped along in a state of dull pain. Maggie, carrying both harmonica and cigarette box, was in a state of pure shock. Manhattan made Dakar look like a country village. She'd never seen anything like it. The buildings were so tall and thickly clustered that, as the daylight waned, their view of the sunset was blocked out entirely.

A few miles away, on the west side of Manhattan, Montague had a spiffy view of the sunset. He'd spent the day collecting his mother's berries and feathers in the park, and after dropping them off at home he'd slipped back out to check the docks. He knew that Aunt Elizabeth had been gone only a week and a day—he'd been counting the hours—and that she'd said it would take two weeks to go to Africa and back. But he was so anxious for her return that he couldn't resist checking, in case maybe she caught an extra-fast ship or something. Twice since she'd left, Isabel had helped him collect his mother's supplies, and on another occasion he'd had dinner in the Moberly-Rats' fancy crate on Wharf 62. But there would be no more snuggling or tail twining with Isabel till the wedding took place.

It was a gorgeous sunset—the sky over New Jersey was streaked bayberry-red and boysenberry-purple—

but Montague's attention was fixed on a ship steaming toward the dock where he was perched. His hopes rose once the ship was tied to and a crane started unloading burlap sacks, for the sacks smelled of coffee beans, and coffee beans struck him as the kind of cargo that might come from Africa. The fourth sack to land on the dock had a scroungy-looking rat lounging on top of it. Montague scurried over and asked if the ship was from Africa.

The scroungy fellow laughed scornfully. "Stupid gringo-rat," he muttered.

That was the only ship in sight, so Montague slumped home to his smoky sewer. As usual, the ratlings were screeching away while his parents worked obliviously on their hats and castles. But in time his mother deserted her dye vats to set out a cold dinner, and once the ratlings had something in their bellies, they dozed off. Montague climbed into his nest, too. But as soon as he closed his eyes, he was back under the laurel bush with Isabel. He missed her too much to sleep.

After his mother finally went to bed, Montague crept out of his nest and dragged a seashell, his latest work in progress, over to a fire smoldering under one of her vats. The half-finished painting was of the laurel bush. The only sounds in the sewer were hissing embers and his father whistling up on his muddy slope, and as Montague carefully applied dyes to the shell with the nib of a sharpened feather, he whistled softly, too, feeling a little less lonely.

It was after midnight before he became drowsy. He set the shell aside and padded down the sewer pipe to a puddle of rainwater.

"Why, Monty, how sweet of you to stay up to greet us!" a familiar voice echoed down the pipe. "I figured we'd have to tiptoe in to keep from waking the household."

Montague let out a cry of delight that did just that— woke the household (if you could call the Mad-Rats' sewer a household). "Aunt Elizabeth! You're back!"

"Yes, and here's your cousin, Maggie. Didn't I tell you Monty was mad for painting, dear? Washing the paint off his paws in the middle of the night! A true artist."

"Hello, Monty," Maggie said.

"Hello, Maggie," said Montague. "Welcome to New York."

"Thank you."

Even in the murky pipe Montague could see that his

young she-rat cousin had inherited her mother's exotic looks. She had a harmonica under one arm and his aunt's cigarette box under the other. He relieved her of her luggage and led the two travelers toward the end of the pipe, where the whole Mad-Rat clan crowded around them.

"Paws a little muddy, miss, so I won't shake," said Mr. Mad-Rat, who'd hiked down off his castle-ridden slope. "You're as pretty as 103."

"That's his favorite castle, dear," Mrs. Mad-Rat said.

"To date," Mr. Mad-Rat murmured.

"You know, Maggie, you've got Liza's nose," Mrs. Mad-Rat said. "But you've got, er, or . . ."

"Don't worry," Aunt Elizabeth said. "She knows about her father."

"Ah. I was just going to say she has Moony's ears. Smaller, of course, and very ladylike, but the shape."

"Why, thank you, Aunt."

"I thought you said it was going to take you two weeks, Aunt Elizabeth!" said Montague.

"Sorry to disappoint you," Elizabeth said.

"Disappoint me!"

"All he's talked about since the day you left is you coming back," said Mrs. Mad-Rat.

"Today I even went to the waterfront," Montague confessed. "But there was nothing from Africa. Did your ship dock over in Brooklyn?"

"We didn't come by sea, dear," Aunt Elizabeth said. "We missed our ship—so we flew."

"Flew!" Mrs. Mad-Rat gasped. "Up in the sky?"

"Exactly."

"You poor things," said Mr. Mad-Rat, who only enjoyed being underground in the mud.

"It wasn't all that bad," said Maggie. "We met a warthog who told riddles."

"What's a warthog?" Montague asked.

"I've heard some not-so-bad things about them," Mr. Mad-Rat said. "They go in for mud, right?"

"By the look of him," Elizabeth said.

"You play this, Maggie?" Montague asked, admiring the harmonica.

"Not very well, but—"

"Don't believe her," said Elizabeth. "She plays it like a Rativarius. I'm only sorry Moony never got to hear her. I'm sure she inherited her musical talent from him."

"Do you sing, too, Maggie?" Montague asked. "Your father sang."

"I sing a little."

"Oh, do give us a song, dearie," Mrs. Mad-Rat said. "Something from Africa."

"I'd love to, Aunt, but I'm a little worn out from the trip. We slept on the flight, but getting in from the airport took forever. This city's endless!"

But the ratlings all chanted "Song! Song!" So Maggie finally picked up her harmonica and started playing a strange, rhythmic tune. She faced away from the mud castles, and when she set the harmonica down, the rhythm kept going, echoing down the sewer pipe as an accompaniment to her voice:

Up the muddy Congo,
Watch for flying spear;
In the muddy water
Creature disappear.

Up the muddy Congo,
Funny atmosphere;
Parrot very noisy,
Have to block your ear.

Up the muddy Congo,
Careful careful steer;
Many many danger
Very very near.

As she sang, the ratlings hopped up and down like jumping beans, and when she stopped singing, they set up such a howl that she sang a few more verses. Mrs. Mad-Rat did a little jig, and even Mr. Mad-Rat got into the act, drumming the sides of an empty vat and joining in every time Maggie got to "muddy." Montague stood next to his aunt, tapping a paw happily to the beat. It would have been even better if Isabel could have been there, but he had a big smile on his snout anyway, for now that his aunt and cousin had arrived, the wedding could take place.

Randal Reese-Rat had a smile on his snout, too, when he woke up the next day. After two weird, woozy weeks in bed, drifting in and out of consciousness, Randal could tell the poison had finally worked its way through his system.

He was tucked in a slipper in his family's crate: crate 8, Wharf 62. He was in the guest room instead of up in his own attic room so his mother wouldn't have to climb too many stairs while looking after him—though in truth he wouldn't have let them take him up to his room anyway. He kept a padlock, picked up from a pack rat, on his door and never let anyone in, not his sister, not even his parents.

Hearing them scurrying around the crate, Randal wondered if they'd had breakfast yet. He actually had a bit of an appetite for a change. He threw back the covers and stood up out of the slipper. Though he felt a little dizzy, he didn't keel over. He made his way to a piece of mirror propped against the wall. He'd clearly lost weight during his illness, but his fur had a decent gloss to it, and, if it was slightly out of place, that could be taken care of as soon as he got upstairs to his trusty toothbrush. His tail was looking a bit skinny, too—and there was a Band-Aid on it, covering the greenish splotch left by the poison. His instinct had been to black out the splotch with a felt pen, but his sister, Ellie, had talked him into the Band-Aid.

"You don't have such a nice long tail as Montague Mad-Rat," she'd said, "but now at least you have a war wound. She-rats love war wounds."

Just hearing the name Montague Mad-Rat had set Randal's teeth on edge, but he'd decided Ellie might be right about the war wound. Not that he needed anything like a war wound to win Isabel Moberly-Rat back from a sewer-dwelling shell painter. After all, he *was* a Reese-Rat. Moreover, it was a well-known fact that he and Isabel were intended for each other. And she'd always been putty in his paws. When he thought the poison was going to kill him, he'd finally proposed to her—the idea of dying all alone had scared him—and she jumped at the chance. But last week he'd made a tragic blunder. A bedraggled, foul-smelling she-rat had paid him a sickroom visit and he'd sent her packing. How could he have known it was Izzy? Izzy was always clean and proper, and always wore a blue ribbon around her neck, whereas this rat was ribbonless and utterly disgusting.

Now he had only a week to win her back. In a week, according to Ellie, a member of that crazy Mad-Rat clan was arriving from some ratforsaken place and then Isabel would marry the upstart—turning him, Randal Reese-Rat, into an object of pity throughout ratdom.

Unthinkable.

But now at least he felt strong enough to launch his campaign. He wished he had more time. In a month or so all this hero worshipping of the sewer rat, all this excitement about saving the wharves, would blow over, and Isabel would come to her senses and realize she had married beneath her. As things stood, Randal would have to work quickly.

Was it too early to pay Isabel a visit right now? He figured it was still before nine, for his mother hadn't knocked yet, and she'd been coming in every morning around nine to try to get him to nibble some cheese. He peered out a slit between two of the crate's slats—and blinked in surprise. The western end of Wharf 62 was an enormous bank of windows, and as the day went on, more and more light poured in. Judging by the brightness, it was already eleven o'clock, maybe even noon.

Randal crept out of the guest room and poked his head into the living room just as his parents were about to walk out the front crack of the crate. He expected them to screech in delight at his recovery, but they managed to contain themselves.

"Oh, Randal," Mrs. Reese-Rat said, looking more flustered than overjoyed.

Mr. Reese-Rat cleared his throat. "Look at you, son, up and about."

"I guess I missed breakfast," said Randal.

"We didn't want to disturb you today, honey," Mrs. Reese-Rat said.

"Why? It's the first day I've actually felt like eating."

"Come on you guys, we'll be late!" This was Ellie, yelling from outside the crate.

"Where are you going?" Randal asked.

Again Mr. Reese-Rat cleared his throat uncomfortably. "Well, son, the truth is we're going to Isabel's wedding."

"Isabel's wedding!"

"Up on the great pier," said Mrs. Reese-Rat.

"But she's not getting married for another week!"

"Change of plans, apparently," said Mr. Reese-Rat. "I'm sorry, son. I know how hard this must be on you."

"That's why we didn't want to disturb you, love. We wouldn't even be attending ourselves, but with Ellie the she-rat of honor . . ."

"And me serving in the rat cabinet with Hugh," said Mr. Reese-Rat, referring to Isabel's father.

Mrs. Reese-Rat came over and gave Randal's paw a squeeze. "Poor baby. Why don't you just climb back into bed? As soon as we get back, I'll fix you some nice cheese fondue to buck up your spirits."

"Remember, son, disappointment strengthens a rat's spine. There may come a day when you'll be able to remember this setback and smile."

This was unbearable. Yet Randal managed to yawn and let his eyelids droop, as if the whole matter bored him. "I couldn't care less," he said, turning away.

But in fact he was grinding his teeth. If his own parents pitied him this way—*poor baby*, indeed!—imagine how the rest of the rat world would treat him! He could just hear the whispers: "Oh, look, there's that pathetic Randal Reese-Rat who lost Isabel Moberly-Rat to the sewer dweller." It was all so unfair! Everything was conspiring against him lately—and now the wedding was taking place before he could do anything about it!

A minute after his parents left, he crept up to the front crack and peered down the wide aisle that ran between the odd- and even-numbered crates. Wharf 62 appeared to be ratless. Everyone must have gone to the wedding. The only sign of life was a few wisps of smoke curling out of crate 44: the home of Digby Dinner-Rat, no doubt busy preparing the wedding feast.

At the thought of food, Randal ducked into the kitchen and had a bite of breakfast to give him strength. Somehow he had to stop the wedding. Normally he didn't go out without combing his fur and putting on cologne, but there was no time to lose, so he dashed out of the crate and headed straight for the entrance to the wharf.

"Nice to see you back up on your paws, Master Reese-Rat," said the dormouse on duty. "Couldn't miss the great event, eh?"

Randal just grunted, unsure if the runty character was making fun of him or not. As he stepped out of the wharf, he covered his eyes. After two weeks shut up in his crate, the late-summer sun was blinding. Lowering his paw, he squinted at a cloudless sky. Typical of that Mad-Rat's dumb luck, he thought as he crept northward along the edge of the West Side Highway. Perfect weather for his wedding day. Yet maybe it wouldn't turn out so perfectly after all.

In spite of eating breakfast, Randal was still weak, and though the great pier was less than half a mile north of Wharf 62, he had to stop twice along the way to rest. By the time he got there, the pier was so crowded he could barely squeeze onto the near end. Unlike the wharves, the pier was open, with no roof, and there must have been six or seven thousand rats basking in the sunshine—six or seven thousand rats between him and the far end of the pier, where the wedding party was assembled atop a dumpster.

Hooding his eyes, Randal could just make them out. In the middle stood Mr. Moberly-Rat, his bald head catching the sun. To his left, his plump wife. To her left, Isabel, looking more radiant than Randal had ever seen her, with a sparkle in her eye and a brand-new blue ribbon around her neck. Next to her stood Ellie, with an imitation-Izzy ribbon around *her* neck—a green one— probably in hopes that she could catch a husband, too.

On Mr. Moberly-Rat's right, the crazy Mad-Rat clan was gathered: Montague the Upstart, trying to look bashful; an older he-rat caked with mud; an older she-rat in a vulgar purple-feather hat; another older she-rat; a young she-rat leaning on a harmonica, of all things; and a bunch of mewling bratling-ratlings who'd probably never been out of the sewer before in their lives.

As Mr. Moberly-Rat stepped up to the edge of the

dumpster, an expectant silence fell over the vast crowd.

"Welcome, fellow rats," the rat leader cried, and his fine, high-pitched screech produced the usual murmur of admiration. It carried even to Randal, at the very back of the crowd. "We are gathered here today to celebrate the marriage of my daughter, Isabel, to the young rat responsible for the very fact that we are . . . gathered here today."

A shriek of approval rose from the rat multitude.

"We are assembled here," Mr. Moberly-Rat went on redundantly as the shrieking died down, "to wish Isabel and Montague ratspeed on the occasion of their nuptials." His tail twitched first to the left, then to the right. "Honored as I am by the part my daughter played in saving us all from extermination, it wouldn't be suitable for me to sing her praises at too great a length. It would be unseemly for me, her father, to bask in the reflected glory. However, I can have no such qualms about singing the praises of Montague Mad-Rat."

The throng of wedding guests let out a boisterous cheer.

"Montague the Magnificent!" Mr. Moberly-Rat cried. "What can you say about a rat who, with his very own paws, created works of art of such rare quality that human beings were willing to pay a fortune for them? How can we do justice to a rat whose painstakingly painted seashells are of such superb workmanship that members of the very species that wanted to poison us and convert our precious wharves into parking lots have turned around and . . ."

What a phony old windbag, Randal thought bitterly. *Works of art of such rare quality*, indeed! For generations, well-bred wharf rats had held that rats who made things with their own paws were scum. And then along comes this sewer rat with his *painstakingly painted seashells* . . . If only he could somehow shove the whole dumpster off the end of the pier into the Hudson River! But it would take an hour to shoulder his way through the crowd, and even with all their help he wouldn't be able to budge the thing.

"Hey!" Randal cried, feeling a tug on his tail.

"Sorry, buddy, but could you maybe move over a couple of inches? Please?"

Randal peered down at a pint-sized brown rat clinging to a piling, trying to squeeze up onto the pier. Randal hated being touched by strangers, so he made room.

"Thanks!" the brown rat cried ecstatically. "I can't believe I made it! This is so cool!"

Randal yawned.

"Nice key," the brown rat said.

Randal, who wore the key to his padlock on a string around his neck, gave a grunt.

"What's it to?"

"My room."

"Wow, your own room! You wharf rats got it made! Is that them up there? Which one's Montague Mad-Rat?"

"I wouldn't know, or care."

Brown rats are smaller than wharf rats, and their fur isn't as sleek. This one was so small he had to bounce up and down to get a view of the rats on the dumpster. "Is that him, with his tail around the she-rat's? She's a looker, isn't she? But, then, he deserves the best."

Randal saw that Montague Mad-Rat and Isabel were now standing with their tails twined—right in public! This was too much. It was worse than the rat poison. And there was absolutely nothing he could do about it! Even if he'd been at his healthiest, he couldn't have made himself heard on the dumpster, for he didn't have one of those fine, screechy voices like Isabel's father.

Since the farce of a wedding was going to happen no matter what he did, Randal saw no point in torturing himself further, so he jumped off the pier and headed back down the edge of the West Side Highway, wishing he'd never gotten out of bed in the first place.

Losing one audience member out of thousands didn't faze Mr. Moberly-Rat for a second.

"As the old saying goes, my fellow rats, it's an ill wind that doesn't blow *some* rat good!" he cried. "Even unhappy events can have happy outcomes. One such unhappy event was the loss earlier this week of our beloved friend and neighbor, Miss Spinster-Rat, one of the eldest known rats in ratdom. We all mourn her—and will long remember her charity to rats less fortunate than herself, as well as her generosity when it came to her remarkable collection of soda pops. However, when she crossed the gulf to the land of dead rats, her former home came onto the market. Her dwelling place—crate 6—became available.

"We all know how hard it is to find quality crates in New York City, so Lavinia and I took the liberty of snapping up crate 6 for the newlyweds. My original intention was to offer them a section of our own crate—crate 11, just across the way—but as my dear wife very rightly pointed out"—here Mr. Moberly-Rat cast a smile on his overweight wife—"as Lavinia most wisely brought to my attention, Isabel and Montague are now a couple and need a place of their own. Number 6 is a nice-sized crate, quite spacious. So if by any chance some little grandratlings come along, there will be plenty of room." Mr. Moberly-Rat winked at the young couple, oblivious of the blushes at the tips of their ears. "And now, my good rats, let us bring these joyous festivities to a close. I declare that Montague and Isabel are joined together in holy ratrimony."

"Ratified!" six or seven thousand rats cried out in unison.

Randal, who was now nearly to Wharf 62, had missed Mr. Moberly-Rat's concluding remarks, but this last cry was too loud not to hear—and he knew all too well what it meant. "That kills me," he muttered.

He was almost a prophet. A human truck driver, startled by the mysterious, high-pitched screech, drove his truck up on the curb of the West Side Highway and missed Randal by a whisker. And while Randal didn't get flattened, he did get splattered, for the truck's tires slid off the curb and landed right in a mud puddle.

"That was quick, Master Reese-Rat," said the dormouse as Randal slouched up to the wharf. "Wet wedding?"

"Unspeakable," Randal snapped.

When he got into crate 8, he dragged himself up the stairs, unlocked his padlock, and locked himself into his room. He headed straight for his bathroom, where he pulled the paper clip off the end of the rubber siphon tube he'd rigged for a shower. Once he'd scrubbed every inch of his fur three times over, he got out and dried himself with a gym sock he'd picked up from a pack rat who'd pilfered it from a sidewalk sock vender. After replacing the soggy Band-Aid with a fresh one, Randal spent a good fifteen minutes combing his fur with his beloved toothbrush. He used to carry the toothbrush around with him everywhere, to touch up his fur if it got blown out of place, but Ellie had convinced him to leave it at home.

"She-rats don't like he-rats who are *too* well-groomed," she said.

How a rat could be *too* well-groomed, Randal couldn't imagine, but since he'd begun leaving the

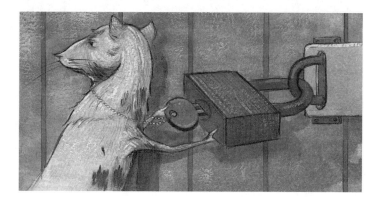

toothbrush at home, there was no denying more she-rats were batting their beady eyes at him. Ellie had also advised him against using too much cologne. She-rats, she claimed, didn't like he-rats who smelled too perfumy. So lately he'd been putting just half a drop behind each ear before going out. If nothing else, this would make his bottle of cologne—a sample some pack rat had snitched out of a postman's sack—last longer. But after the ordeal of the wedding and the mud puddle, he couldn't resist giving himself a good dousing, even though he hadn't the slightest intention of going out. All he wanted to do was lie down and *not* think about the humiliation of having thousands of rats witness Isabel choosing that miserable Mad-Rat over him.

So Randal lay back on his pillow and let his eyes roam around his room. And, miraculously, the horde of rats faded quickly from his thoughts, giving way to herds of zebras and flocks of whooping cranes and packs of timber wolves. How wonderful to be back among his wild animal friends after all this time! For ever since falling ill he'd been deprived of the secret collection of photographs that papered his walls and ceiling.

Though Randal's father was one of New York City's leading rats, his grandfather, Gregory Reese-Rat, had been even more famous. His grandfather, who had once found a wallet stuffed with twenty-dollar bills by a curb, had been known as Gregory the Great.

One of Randal's earliest and happiest memories was of his distinguished, well-to-do grandfather pulling him around the back of crate 8.

"There's something I want to show you, Randal," Gregory Reese-Rat had said.

"What is it, Granddad?" the little ratling asked, staring wide-eyed at his grandfather's paws.

"It's not on me, my boy."

"Where is it, Granddad?"

"Be ready at two a.m. I'll show you."

Two a.m.! Young Randal had never been up past ten. He went up to bed at eight-thirty, as usual, and soon his mother came up to kiss him good night (back then there was no padlock on his door). But he was much too excited to sleep. Hours later, when his grandfather slipped into his room with an empty plastic sandwich bag over his shoulder, Randal was ready and waiting.

He followed his grandfather out past the dozing night dormouse, across the West Side Highway and north along the edge of Eighth Avenue. Randal didn't ask where they were going. His legs were still very short, and it was all he could do to keep up. But after crossing dozens of streets, his grandfather finally stopped in front of a structure that must have been ten times the size of Wharf 62.

"What's that?" Randal asked, panting.

"Madison Square Garden," said Gregory Reese-Rat. "Or so they call it."

"The human beings?"

His grandfather nodded. "Remember, Randal, you never want to come here any earlier than this. They congregate here by the thousands, and you might get trampled."

The place was locked up, but Gregory Reese-Rat squeezed in under one of many doors. Randal followed with ease.

"What do they do in here, Granddad?" he asked as they pattered up a long, curving ramp.

"You wouldn't believe it if I told you."

"Oh, tell me!"

"Well, most of them scream and clap and stomp

their feet while a few others bounce balls on the floor or smack a rat-sized thingamajig around the ice."

"Why do they do that?" Randal squeaked.

"Religious ceremonies. Part of the ceremony involves exchanging money for food at these altars." Gregory Reese-Rat pointed out one of the food altars. "You've seen the dogs human beings walk around the sidewalks and parks on leashes?"

"Sure."

"Well, humans raise them to be religious sacrifices. They cook them and grind them into sausages and eat them piping hot in bits of bread. Hot dogs, they call them. You ought to hear it when the priests start yelling, 'Get yer hot dogs here!' Makes your fur crawl."

"I was always scared of dogs, Granddad. But now I feel sorry for them."

"As well you might. Imagine being kept on a leash all the time, only to end up being cooked and eaten! Anyway, if you look under the altars, you're apt to find coins. That's when this bag I brought comes in handy. Once I found so many nickels I had to hide three and come back for them the next night."

"What's this funny stuff, Granddad? It doesn't smell good."

"It's called straw, Randal." The ramp had led them up to a broad arcade where the concrete floor was covered with straw.

"I don't like it. It musses up your fur."

Watching the young rat use his tail to flick bits of straw off himself made the old rat chuckle. "You're one for the books, Randal. First thing you did when you were born was start licking yourself clean. Neatest ratling I ever saw."

"What's this nasty old straw for?"

"It's the reason I brought you here tonight."

"This is what you wanted to show me?"

"In a way, yes. You see, they don't use straw for their usual ceremonies, but every year around this time they take time out for a different kind of religious ritual. It involves more than just dog-eating. They cart creatures in from the ends of the earth and torture them."

"Torture them?"

"They snap whips at them and make them parade around and jump through hoops."

"Why do they do that, Granddad?"

"It's the humans' way of demonstrating to themselves how powerful they are," the old rat said knowledgeably. "And an utterly terrifying spectacle it is."

"Do they make rats jump through hoops?" Randal squeaked in dismay.

"Fortunately, they go in for larger, less refined creatures. Dreadful-looking brutes like lions and elephants."

"What are lions and elephants?"

"I could show you, but I don't think you'd—"

"Show me, Granddad! Where are they?"

"When they're not torturing them, the humans keep them locked up in pens and cages."

Gregory Reese-Rat led Randal across the straw-covered floor to the other end of the dim arcade.

"P.U.," Randal said.

"Those there are called horses," Gregory Reese-Rat said as they scuttled by a stable.

"I've seen horses, Granddad. Police-people ride them in the streets."

"But have you seen one like him?"

"Not with all those stripes."

"He's called a zebra, I believe. They torture him like

the horses—by putting a piece of metal in his mouth and yanking him around by it. Now, Randal, prepare yourself. Some of these other beasts are even uglier than human beings."

They came to a row of towering cages. Curled up asleep in the first cage were several creatures that actually resembled human beings—though they at least had some fur.

"What are they?" Randal gasped.

"Monkeys, they're called."

"And what's that?" Randal said, gaping at an enormous heap of fur in the next cage.

"That's called a bear. They torture her by making her walk on a big ball. If she falls off, they snap their whips at her."

"No wonder she's so exhausted."

"Seen enough?"

"No!"

"But you're getting covered with straw."

Randal quickly flicked himself clean with his tail. He was surprised at himself. For a minute there he'd actually forgotten about his fur.

"Come on now, Randal, let's go. You'll end up having nightmares and I'll catch it from your mother."

"But what's that one? It's like a huge alley cat with a hairy neck."

"That's a male lion. Gruesome, isn't he?"

Randal crept toward the cage, mesmerized. To him the enormous sleeping cat wasn't gruesome at all.

"Randal, get back!"

Randal obediently jumped back. "What's wrong, Granddad?"

"If you woke him, he'd slap a paw through those bars and make mousemeat out of you. They're as ferocious as they are ugly, those beasts."

In the end Gregory Reese-Rat had to drag his grandratling away from the cages. He'd always thought of Randal as a bit of a scaredy-rat—and here he was creeping right up to cages with lions and tigers in them!

Back at the other end of the long arcade, Gregory Reese-Rat stubbed his left front paw on something. It was painful—that paw was getting arthratic—but he smiled proudly as he pulled a quarter out of the straw.

"This is why I brought you tonight," he said, "not to look at a bunch of monsters. You see? They call this temple of theirs Madison Square *Garden* because the pickings are always so good. But they're especially good during their special ritual. The straw, you see. They put it down on account of the beasts. But what happens is, if the humans drop money, they don't hear it, then the straw covers it up. It's a regular gold mine. Only a handful of rats know anything about it. Fact is, I never even told your father. But what with feeling more and more rickety lately, and one thing and another, I figured . . . well, it would be a shame for my best financial tips to die with me."

Randal was horrified to think of his grandfather dying. At the same time, though, he was honored that the great rat would choose him over his father to pass his trade secrets on to. But when he finally climbed onto his pillow at dawn and fell asleep, Randal didn't dream about quarters or shiny new dimes. He dreamt about monkeys and bears and zebras and lions.

So it was that Randal's strange fascination with other species was awakened. He kept it top secret, of course. Rats are extremely rat-centric, believing themselves to be superior to other species, so his odd interest would have made him a laughingstock. The only rat who might have suspected him was his grandfather, and not long after that remarkable night in Madison Square Garden, Gregory Reese-Rat sent Randal and his family into mourning by crossing the gulf into the land of dead rats.

Since then, Randal had had just two close calls.

The first was at the zoo. As soon as he reached the age when wharf rats are allowed to go out and about by themselves, Randal started sneaking up to the zoo in Central Park. There he could marvel at—and sometimes even chat with—the most remarkable creatures imaginable, from baboons in jungle habitats to penguins who lived on a mound of paw-numbing ice. He occasionally ran into other rats there, but never any wharf rats—at least not until a crisp fall afternoon when he bumped into Bernie Bat-Rat near the sea lions' tank. Bernie was a bully who, like his fathers before him, usually carried a stick. But that day he'd left it home in favor of a paper bag.

"Hey, Bernie," Randal said nervously. "What's up?"

"Collecting cash for the Rat Rent, of course. You?"

"Same."

"Where's your bag?"

"It blew away, darn it."

"Well, if you'd leave that stupid toothbrush at home, Reese-Rat, you might be able to keep hold of your bag. There's probably one in that trash can. I'll keep you covered while you look."

So poor Randal had to set down his toothbrush and climb into a trash can while Bernie kept an eye out for alley cats. Randal emerged from the foul-smelling rubbish with a crumpled wax-paper bag and a wad of chewing gum in his fur. It took over an hour with his toothbrush to get the gum out, and for days afterward dirt kept sticking to that patch of fur. But at least Bernie hadn't learned his secret.

His other close shave had come early one Thursday morning last spring. He was trying to tug a certain yellow-spined magazine out of a bundle of magazines in front of a rat-colored town house on Horatio Street. Horatio Street wasn't far from Wharf 62, and Randal had learned that a human being who lived in the rat-colored town house there subscribed to a magazine that often featured wild-animal photos. He'd also learned that the humans in that neighborhood put out their recyclables on Wednesday nights, so early on Thursday mornings he slipped over there. But this particular morning he'd worked the yellow magazine only halfway out of the tight bundle when he was startled by a familiar voice.

"Gad, Randal, what are you doing?"

"Izzy!" he said, letting go of the magazine's yellow spine. "What are you doing out so early?"

"I must have spring fever, I couldn't sleep," said Isabel Moberly-Rat. "How about you?"

"Same."

Isabel eyed him suspiciously. Randal was usually so bored by things, she couldn't imagine him having spring fever. "What are you doing with that magazine?"

"I needed some more stuffing for my pillow. It's gotten a little flat. Thought I'd use some paper."

"Oh. I'll help you."

Together they pulled the magazine out of the bundle.

"Gad, look at that awful thing!" she said, averting her eyes from the picture of an elephant on the cover. "A tail in front and back!"

"Don't worry," said Randal, who was on a first-name basis with an African elephant named Mauri up at the zoo. "When the paper's crumpled up in the pillowcase, it won't matter what's on it."

"If I help you carry that magazine back to your crate, will you finally let me see your room?"

"It's a pigsty, Izzy."

"Are you sure? You're the neatest rat I know, but you always say your room's such a mess."

Randal yawned. "Maybe I'll clean it up one day, but cleaning's such a bore. Is that a fresh ribbon?"

"Mm," she said, touching the blue ribbon at her neck. "I just changed it yesterday."

"It has a nice sheen to it."

"Thanks, Randal. Here, I'll help you carry it, even if I can't see your room."

Usually he leafed through the yellow magazine right there on the sidewalk and ripped out the photos he liked best, but that morning Isabel helped him lug the whole thing back to crate 8. After promising to drop by crate 11 for a visit later, he dragged the magazine up to his room. Most of his wall and ceiling space was already taken. The walls were devoted to photos of gazelles and pythons and giraffes and zebras and two-toed sloths hanging upside down from limbs and beavers gnawing tree trunks and elephants with gigantic tusks and hyenas and moose and timber wolves and weasels. The ceiling was reserved for birds: toucans and whooping cranes and a peregrine falcon and a huge flock of flamingos in flight and a bald eagle with what looked uncomfortably like a rat, but was actually a prairie dog, in its talons. As for the female emperor penguin, he hadn't been quite sure if she was a bird or not, so he'd pasted her photo at the top of the wall, wrapping around onto the ceiling.

Over time Randal had become very selective about what he put up. He'd reached the point where he rejected entire issues of the yellow magazine. But in the middle of this latest issue there was an irresistible photo of a saddle-billed stork, which he carefully ripped out and stuck up between the flamingos and the falcon.

On the afternoon of Isabel's wedding, however, he spent little time looking at the stork. Or at the falcon.

Or at the flamingos. He was too busy concentrating on
the bald eagle. He pictured the majestic bird of
prey swooping down over the wedding ceremony and
snatching Montague Mad-Rat off the dumpster. Then
he pictured the eagle flying out over New York Harbor,
Montague struggling free, Montague tumbling through
the air and getting pierced on the tip of the torch on
the Statue of Liberty. He pictured the great bird dropping Montague somewhere in the middle of the
Atlantic Ocean, hundreds of miles from shore. Or taking him to a ledge on top of a skyscraper and gob-
bling him up for dinner. Or flying him home to a

faraway nest and divvying him up to feed his young.

Once all the eagle possibilities were exhausted, Randal dropped his eyes to his picture of elephants and imagined himself arriving at the pier on the back of his massive friend, Mauri. Of course this was stretching fantasy to its limits. Mauri was severely depressed, and the only time he so much as stood up was when the zookeeper prodded him with a long pole to make him move from his indoor cage to his outdoor pen. In fact, Mauri was a big baby, always moaning about missing his mother. But Randal conveniently put that out of his mind. He imagined the horrified screeches as Mauri clumped out through the crowd of wedding guests— then the stunned silence when he and Mauri stopped just in front of the dumpster. "Chuck out the garbage, Mauri!" he would cry, and the giant beast would lower his tusks and flick the dumpster and everyone on it into the Hudson River.

These daydreams had such a soothing effect on Randal that he closed his eyes and fell into a rat nap. Since he wasn't a hundred percent recovered, and since it had been a very trying day, he probably would have slept straight through till the next morning if he hadn't been rudely awakened by a commotion right outside his crate.

Rats sleep deeply, and it took Randal a moment to orient himself. Blinking, he realized it was now nighttime. The only light leaking between the slats in the crate was feeble electric light from the lightbulbs the human wharf owner brought every year when he collected his rent.

The hubbub, Randal realized, was cheering.

"Not more Mad-Ratting," he moaned, rolling off his pillow and stumbling over to his viewing slit.

Directly below, just outside the entrance crack to old Miss Spinster-Rat's place, stood none other than the wretched upstart, his paw slung over Isabel's shoulder. Randal squeezed his eyes shut and pinched himself, hoping to wake himself up from this nightmare. But when he reopened his eyes, the newlyweds were still down there, waving to a cheering crowd.

When the cheering died down, the upstart piped up in a quiet, phonily shy voice: "I, uh, I just want to thank you all for making this the greatest day of my life."

"Our lives," Isabel chimed in.

"Our lives," Montague corrected himself, holding her tighter. "The wedding ceremony was really something."

"It was stupendous," Isabel said.

"Stupendous," Montague echoed her (dumb cluck that he was, Randal thought). "And now having this beautiful crate to live in, it's . . . it's—"

"It's just perfect!" Isabel cried. "Thanks, Mom and Dad—and thank you, everybody else! It's like a dream come true."

Randal staggered back as if he'd been kicked in the gut. Isabel and the rat who'd stolen her away from him were going to live right next door!

Tripping on his toothbrush, Randal fell splat on his back—right on his tail injury. His pillow was only inches away, but he just rolled over with a groan and lay there on the floor with his face in his paws, wishing with all his heart that he could crawl into a pouch and disappear like the baby kangaroo at the Central Park Zoo.

As soon as the wedding guests had shown the newlyweds their new home, hundreds of snouts began to twitch, and hundreds of pairs of beady eyes began to check crate 44, home of Digby Dinner-Rat.

As a youngster, Digby had gone out scouring the streets for coins like other self-respecting wharf rats. Anxious to make a name for himself, he'd been very daring, often risking his tail as he dashed onto a crowded sidewalk to retrieve a dime or nickel to contribute to the Rat Rent. Then one day he was pattering along the rail of the local subway line when a dollar bill came fluttering down from the platform. There were no vibrations in the rail, so Digby knew the local train wasn't coming, which meant he had plenty of time to catch the glorious prize. But a current of air swept the bill out of his reach. It floated off beyond some sooty girders, and as he raced after it, it never entered his head that he was running onto the express tracks—or that the current of air might have been caused by an oncoming express train.

The next thing Digby knew, he was on his back in bed in crate 44, looking up at his widowed mother's tear-streaked face. As he tried to get up, the tragic truth hit him. His left hind leg was missing. It had been squished by the express train, and a general ratitioner had had to amputate.

After that, Digby refused to leave his bed. His poor mother waited on him paw and foot, but she couldn't convince him that his life hadn't reached a dead end. What good was a rat with only one hind leg? Finally, at her wits' end, Mrs. Dinner-Rat worked up the courage to approach the great Hugh Moberly-Rat with her problem.

The famed rat dropped by crate 44 to give Digby a pep talk. Mr. Moberly-Rat was as wordy and repetitive as usual, but Digby listened attentively, conscious of the honor of the visit.

"Do you know why you're called Dinner-Rat, Digby?" the great rat asked. "Are you aware of the source of your name?"

"Mom says Dad's grandfather used to make dinner for lots of rats, or something like that. So rats started calling him Dinner-Rat and it stuck."

"Your great-grandfather was a first-rate cook—a master chef. My own grandfather used to rave about his macaroni and cheese. Utterly sublime, he called it.

And do you know the great thing about being a cook, Digby? There's no need for scurrying around. You can pretty much stay put. You need your paws, of course, for stirring. But hind legs hardly play a part in it."

And so, encouraged by this rat leader, Digby decided to get out of bed and turn himself into a chef. Instead of copying his great-grandfather's famous recipe, he made up his own masterpiece, a dish of cooked vegetables and melted mozzarella cheese called ratatouille. Rats clamored for Digby's ratatouille. But he only made it on special occasions.

No occasion could have been more special than the marriage of the daughter of Hugh Moberly-Rat, the rat who'd changed Digby's life. So Digby took special pains with the ratatouille he made for the wedding feast. He served it in the wide aisle that ran down the center of the wharf, and the guests all sang—or rather screeched—his praises.

Except for the Mad-Rats. The Mad-Rats had re-markably little interest in food. They had to eat to stay alive, of course. But their meals weren't regular, and none of them—not Mr. or Mrs. Mad-Rat or Aunt Eliz-abeth—cared what they put in their mouths so long as it gave them enough energy to pursue their castle building and hatmaking and traveling. So while most of the wedding guests ate Digby's ratatouille slowly, to savor the flavor, the Mad-Rats wolfed theirs down. And the instant they were finished, they excused them-selves to go home. It had been amusing for Mr. and Mrs. Mad-Rat to venture aboveground and witness their son's marriage to a pretty young she-rat from a fancy wharf family, but they were itching to get back to their work, and besides, the ratlings were get-ting cranky. As for Aunt Elizabeth, she was still a little worn out from the trip in from the airport. So they started saying their good-byes right in the middle of the feast.

This disruption naturally got under Digby's fur. And if that wasn't bad enough, there was Maggie Mad-Rat, who took one nibble of ratatouille and stopped eating altogether. Maggie didn't mean to be rude. She'd just never had ratatouille in Africa and didn't much care for the taste. But Digby, who was very touchy and watched everyone carefully, was insulted.

"Want to come home with us, Maggie?" Aunt Eliza-beth asked.

"Maybe I better," Maggie said.

"Oh, but Maggie, you have to stay!" cried Isabel. "The party's just getting started."

"Yes, and you brought your harmonica," said Montague. "I was hoping maybe you'd play something."

"Would you like some dinner music?" said Maggie.

"We'd love it!" cried Isabel.

So while the older Mad-Rats gave the Mad-Ratlings piggyback rides back to the sewer, Maggie remained on Wharf 62. She picked up her harmonica and started playing a jazzy tune. It was an instant hit with the wedding guests, who stopped eating and started tapping their hind feet to the rhythm. Soon every rat on the wharf was tapping a hind foot—every rat except two. One was Digby. He had only one hind foot and needed it for support, but even if he'd had both, he wouldn't have tapped. The other non-tapper was Randal Reese-Rat. He'd squirmed under the pillow up in his bedroom to block out the sounds of the festivities going on below.

After a while Maggie Mad-Rat set down her harmonica and started singing:

> *In the j-j-jungle*
> *The juju-birds are wed,*
> *In a bakawana tree*
> *They make their b-b-bed.*
>
> *Before they fall asleep, though,*
> *The jujus f-f-fly,*

And all the other jujus
J-j-join them in the sky.

After singing these two verses, she took up her harmonica again—and Digby's ratatouille was totally forgotten. Everywhere rats jumped up and started
dancing. The instant Maggie stopped, rats cried out:

"Sing it again!"

"Encore, encore!"

Maggie set down her harmonica and sang the funny
little song again.

After five or six tunes, a few of the older rats strag-
gled off to bed, but the younger ones were so crazy
about Maggie's beat that they made her play till she
could no longer lift her harmonica.

Though Montague had never done much dancing, he
enjoyed himself as much as anyone, but in his heart he
wasn't all that sorry when the party finally broke up. At
last, he would get to be alone with Isabel!

But what about Maggie? Isabel wouldn't hear of her
lugging her harmonica all the way back to the Mad-
Rats' sewer pipe at that late hour.

"But I lugged it all the way from the airport yesterday," she said, "and Mom's suitcase, too."

"All the more reason you shouldn't have to lug it
anymore tonight," said Isabel. "You'll stay over with us
here in our new crate. Right, Monty?"

"Um—"

"Don't be silly, it's your wedding night," Maggie

said, propping her harmonica by their front door. "I'll leave this here and come for it tomorrow before we go to Central Park."

The plan for the next day, barring rain, was for the newlyweds to take Maggie to visit her father's grave.

"You're not going down into the sewers alone at night," Isabel said. "We'll walk you."

"But you don't want to go all that way at this hour."

In the end, Montague came up with a solution: Maggie would spend the night in Isabel's old room in crate 11. He thanked her for the wonderful entertainment and ducked into crate 6, leaving Isabel to walk Maggie across the wharf to her former home.

Ten minutes later, Isabel walked back across the wharf, so noisy and crowded a few minutes earlier, now silent and eerily deserted. Before entering crate 6, she inspected herself in the shiny harmonica. She straightened her ribbon—it had gotten a little wilted while she was dancing—and fluffed up her fur. As she glanced over her shoulder to make sure her ring hadn't slid down her tail, the fur on the back of her neck stood up. What a creepy feeling! Someone was watching her— she was positive. She could feel it.

But before she could locate any spying eyes, Montague burst out through the crack and swept her up in his paws.

"Gad!" she said. "What are you doing?"

"Wharf rats are supposed to carry their wives across the thresholds of their new crates," he said. "Your father told me. I guess I'm going to be living on a wharf now, so I figured I better do it."

Isabel giggled, forgetting all about the creepy feeling, and the happy young couple disappeared into their new crate for their wedding night.

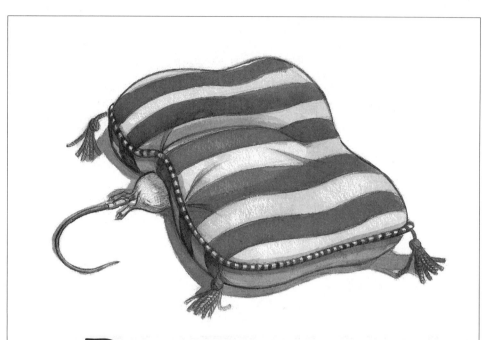

During the singing and dancing Randal had remained burrowed under his pillow. This muffled the noise, but he wasn't used to lying on the hard floor, so he'd been unable to drop off. Through the floor he'd eventually heard his parents come home, soon followed by a knock on his door.

"Are you all right, Randal, sweetie?"

He pulled his head out from under the pillow and said cheerfully, "I'm dandy, Mom, thanks for asking. Not quite a hundred percent yet, but a lot better. Sleep tight." He couldn't stand his parents feeling sorry for him.

He burrowed back under the pillow. A couple of sleepless hours later, he heard Ellie come home and climbed on top of the pillow. Everything was quiet now, so he could finally sleep. But then he heard Isabel's voice and crept over to his slit.

To his surprise and delight, he saw the upstart Mad-Rat duck into crate 6 while Isabel led another she-rat back to her old crate. Had the newlyweds quarreled already? Or maybe Isabel had seen the light? With the dizzy excitement of the wedding over, maybe her head had finally cleared and she'd seen what should have been plain as the snout on her face: that her new husband was unsuitable for her. Suddenly Randal almost felt sorry for her. Imagine, giving up a fine old name like Moberly-Rat to become a Mad-Rat!

He flopped back on his bed, his spirits rising like the bald eagle on his ceiling. Maybe life wasn't so miserable after all. That Mad-Rat would probably spend one night alone in Miss Spinster-Rat's old crate, then slink back to the sewers where he belonged. Then the wedding would just be canceled—de-ratified—since they'd never even spent a night together. A marriage didn't count unless you cuddled up together for a night. And once Isabel was single again . . .

He heard pawsteps and crept back to the slit. Isabel was returning to crate 6—alone! She stopped in front of that stupid harmonica to fix her ribbon. She was gussying herself up for the guttersnipe! Then the guttersnipe popped out the front crack and lifted Isabel right off her feet. It was all Randal could do not to let out a screech.

But he didn't. He didn't move a muscle. Long after the newlyweds vanished into crate 6, he remained at his slit, glaring out into the night without so much as blinking an eye, his hatred and self-pity all but turning him to stone.

Monty? Wake up, Monty!"

Montague grunted drowsily. He'd been having the nicest dream of snuggling with Isabel.

"Do you smell smoke, Monty?"

"Mmm," he said sleepily. "Mom's dye vats."

"What? What are you talking about?"

"The fires under the vats." He opened one eye. "Izzy?"

"Monty, we're in our new crate! There aren't any dye vats." Montague's other eye opened. He was lying on a plush velvet cushion. Isabel was sitting up beside him, her lovely snout quivering, her ribbon draped over the bedside spool.

"I'm going to check," she cried, slipping out of bed.

He followed her groggily into the hallway. It was smokier there, smokier even than the sewer pipe. As they came out into the front room, Isabel let out a shriek. Flames were dancing in the front crack.

"Is there a back way out?" Montague gasped, instantly wide awake.

They'd been so anxious to cuddle up together they hadn't bothered to explore the crate very thoroughly. But now they dashed down the hallway, past the bedroom door, and found themselves in a good-sized back room that was still pretty much smoke-free. The room was empty except for old Miss Spinster-Rat's things, which had been piled in a corner and covered with a scarf. There was no back crack.

Montague and Isabel locked eyes—and for one long moment they thought exactly the same thing: at least they'd gotten to curl up together on the cushion *once* before they got fried. But rats, especially young ones, have a remarkably strong survival instinct. If cornered by larger animals like dogs or cats, they bare their teeth and fight to the death.

Unfortunately, fires are rarely intimidated by bared teeth. "What should we do?" Montague whispered hoarsely.

Isabel peered around the dim room. Not long ago, she'd been in a surprisingly similar situation, when the gallery owner's assistants had tried to get the shell money back by smoking her and Uncle Moony and Pembroke Pack-Rat out of the gallery walls with poison gas. So she didn't panic now. "Maybe we could pry our way out the back," she said.

They searched the back wall for pawholds. There were several cracks between the slats of wood. But they couldn't pry any of the slats out, even when they counted to three and pulled together. Crate 6 was one of the most solidly constructed crates on the entire wharf.

Smoke began to sift into the back room.

"Maybe we can smother the fire with the cushion," Montague said.

They darted to the hall. But the flames had already reached the bedroom.

"Gad!" said Isabel. "Maybe we can find a crowbar or something."

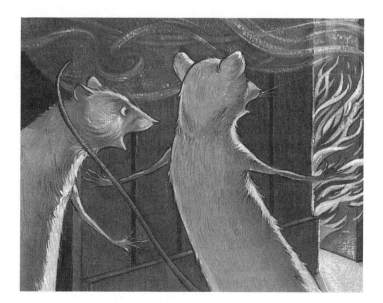

She bolted over to the pile of Miss Spinster-Rat's things and yanked off the scarf. Not a crowbar in sight. Only Miss Spinster-Rat's famous collection of soda pops. There were cans of every kind of cola and un-cola imaginable, all no doubt acquired through a pack-rat supplier. Montague grabbed one can, and Isabel grabbed another. Rolling them over to the doorway shook up the contents, so when the newlyweds aimed the cans down the hallway and yanked the tabs with their teeth, soda fizzed out into the oncoming flames.

It took twelve cans, but they finally put the fire out.

By the time a sticky Montague and a sticky, ribbonless Isabel came slumping out the charred front crack of crate 6, half the sharp-nosed population of Wharf 62 was gathered outside.

"Are you all right?" screeched Hugh Moberly-Rat. "Are either of you injured?"

"We're okay," said Isabel. "But we were just about burnt to a crisp."

"You lit a candle for atmosphere, right?" Ellie Reese-Rat guessed. "Then you got distracted."

"Really!" her father, Clarence, humphed. "It could have spread to us next door."

"But we didn't light any candles!" Isabel said.

"Then how'd it start?" Clarence Reese-Rat demanded.

"We don't have a clue," said Montague. "We were sound asleep."

"You poor dears must be famished after all that fire-fighting," said Mrs. Moberly-Rat. "Here, I brought you some nice Monterey Jack."

In fact, Mrs. Moberly-Rat had snatched the cheese on her way out as a sort of late midnight snack for herself, but she broke off pieces for the two firefighters. Maggie Mad-Rat, who'd followed Mr. and Mrs. Moberly-Rat over from crate 11, wiped the sleep out of her eyes and crept up to the harmonica leaning by the charred crack. The instrument was mostly metal, and though the stops were wooden, they were made of a very hard wood that didn't seem to have suffered much from the flames.

"Still hot," she said, picking it up.

While she blew out a few notes, everyone else's attention turned to something that had been hidden behind the harmonica. A pile of curled, blackened matchsticks.

"Mercy!" cried Mrs. Moberly-Rat. "A firebug!"

"Very suspicious," said Mr. Reese-Rat, peering closely at the evidence. "Pity, the pawprints are burnt away."

"There aren't any firebugs on Wharf 62!" cried a voice in the crowd.

"Never have been!" cried another.

As Maggie continued testing her harmonica, hundreds of pairs of beady eyes turned and fixed on her.

"You didn't go home with the Mad-Rats?" someone asked.

"Where are you from, anyway?

"Africa," Maggie said, setting her harmonica down.

"It's not an African custom, by any chance," said Mr. Reese-Rat, "to incinerate newlyweds?"

Maggie just laughed—and, in spite of being sticky and ribbonless on her wedding night, so did Isabel. "Why on earth would Maggie want to burn us up?" she said. "That's the silliest thing I ever heard of. Where's the night dormouse?"

"Here!" came a squeal from the back of the crowd.

"Let him through," screeched Mr. Moberly-Rat. "Give the dormouse some room."

The crowd parted, and the night dormouse came scurrying up.

"Any strangers come in since midnight?" Mr. Reese-Rat asked sharply.

"No, sir!"

"You're sure you weren't rat napping?"

"I'm a dormouse, sir! I never rat nap! Nobody came in. Only one rat went out in the last few hours."

"And who might that be?"

"Well, Mr. Reese-Rat, sir, it was your son, Randal."

"Randal! When was this?"

"About half an hour ago."

"But it's not even dawn," Mr. Moberly-Rat said, glancing toward the bank of windows at the end of the wharf. "The sun's not even up."

"He goes out early quite a bit, Mr. Moberly-Rat, sir," the night dormouse said.

"He does?" said Mr. Reese-Rat. "Did you know about this, Ellie?"

"Randal's weird," Ellie said with a shrug. "Always was, always will be."

"What does he do out so early, dormouse?" Mr. Reese-Rat asked.

"Search me, sir. But he usually comes back with pieces of shiny paper."

"Shiny paper?"

"He had a big roll of it with him just now when he left. So big he had to drag it."

"Told you he's weird," said Ellie.

"Clarence," Mr. Moberly-Rat said with a heavy sigh. "I don't like to ask you this, old friend, but do you have matches in your crate? Do you happen to keep—"

"Of course we do!" Mr. Reese-Rat snapped. "Everybody does."

Since the crates on the wharf were all made of wood, matches were frowned upon, but wharf rats like the occasional warm meal, so everyone lit occasional fires.

"Now, Hugh," Mr. Reese-Rat said. "I hope you're not implying that Randal had anything to do with this blaze."

"Not at all, not at all. It just struck me as a *little* odd, just a *bit* peculiar, his leaving the wharf at that *particular* moment. Especially considering his former attachment to my daughter."

The tips of Clarence Reese-Rat's ears turned an angry scarlet. But even though he had a good bit of experience at political debate, he couldn't think of a comeback.

"I can't believe Randal would have set our crate on fire," Isabel said. "I mean, he must have known *I* was inside."

Now it was Isabel's ears' turn to redden—though in embarrassment rather than anger, for she realized she'd sounded a little conceited.

"Reese-Rat's never been a regular rat," boomed Bernie Bat-Rat, stepping up with his stick over his shoulder. "Let's check his room. Maybe there's a clue."

"Good luck," said Ellie.

"What do you mean?" Bernie said.

"I mean, he always locks his room."

"He locks his room?" said Mr. Moberly-Rat. "You mean, he bolts the door?"

"He got a padlock," Ellie said. "That's why he wears a key around his neck."

"He always says his room's a mess," said Isabel.

"Dear me," said Mrs. Reese-Rat. "He *is* awfully private about his room."

"Suspicious!" hissed a chorus of rats.

"Come on, guys, let's take a gander," said Bernie, leading a pack of his pals toward crate 8. "We'll knock his door down if we have to."

"Hooligans!" cried Mr. Reese-Rat, blocking his front door. "Did I invite you in?"

"Back off, buster, if you know what's good for you," Bernie said.

"How dare you!"

"Now, Clarence, we all realize this is a difficult situation," Mr. Moberly-Rat interceded. "Quite ticklish, in fact. For my part, I'm sure Randal is innocent of this atrocity—totally blameless. I've always considered him a fine young rat. But perhaps it would be best, in light of his leaving the scene of the crime so—"

"Crime!" cried Mr. Reese-Rat. "Are you actually accusing my son—my son and heir!—of a crime?"

"No one's accusing anyone of anything. But don't you think it would be best, just for the sake of clearing his name, to take a look at—"

But Bernie, sick of diplomacy, simply shoved Mr. Reese-Rat aside and led his pals into crate 8. The

Reese-Rats were right on their heels, Mr. Reese-Rat cursing, Mrs. Reese-Rat tssking, Ellie shouting out directions to her brother's room. Isabel and her parents crowded in after them, as did as many other rats as could squeeze in.

When Bernie reached the door to Randal's attic room, he didn't have to break it down. It wasn't locked. Bernie simply opened it and led the search party inside.

"Dear me," Mrs. Reese-Rat said. "He didn't make his pillow."

This was true. But nothing about the room was suspicious. There was the pillow, and a bedside spool, and a handkerchief rug. The most interesting things there were an open padlock and a half-empty bottle of cologne.

"I wonder why he's so paranoid about letting anyone in here," Ellie said, looking around at the bare walls and ceiling.

"I wouldn't call this messy," Isabel said.

"Yeah, but we're waiting here till he gets back," Bernie said. "Right, boys?"

His pals all agreed.

To the Reese-Rats' dismay, every rat on Wharf 62 barged into crate 8 that day to take a peek at the room of the firebug. Every rat, that is, except Digby Dinner-Rat. Perhaps this was because climbing stairs wasn't much fun with only one hind leg. Or perhaps Digby had other reasons.

While Bernie & Co. spent the day waiting for Randal, Randal spent the day lugging his coiled-up photography collection through storm sewers and broken water mains and subways. Living right next door to the lovey-dovey newlyweds was more than he could stand, so he'd determined to move somewhere he wouldn't have to see, or hear about, the blissful couple.

He had a spot in mind. He loved the Central Park Zoo, and Ellie had mentioned that mangy old Moony Mad-Rat used to work on his rings under the zoo. Since he was dead, the place was bound to be vacant.

It was. But it wasn't very appetizing. After all his exertion, Randal suspected he probably didn't smell very appetizing himself—but this place reeked. It had the sour smell of wine gone bad. Dandelion wine, judging by the residue in the eyedrop bottles scattered around the place. Some of these bottles were broken, too, as

Randal discovered when he got a glass splinter in his right hind foot.

He sat down on a warm pipe to work the splinter out, then he tiptoed carefully around the place. There were numerous signs of habitation, including a saggy cushion, a thimble to hold water, a small crescent wrench, and even some money: a stack of nickels hidden behind an elbow joint. Luckily, there was also a broom. He swept the floor thoroughly and got rid of the empties. Then he uncoiled his photos, inside of which he'd stuck his trusty toothbrush, a supply of fresh Band-Aids, and a dollar bill. He'd wrapped his least favorite photo—of a jackrabbit—around the outside, and it had gotten soiled and damp. But the other photos had weathered the trip nicely, and, famished as he was, he stuck them up on the pipes before venturing out for a nibble.

At that hour the animals in the zoo had all been put inside for the night, and Randal found a number of tasty scraps in their outdoor pens. Once his stomach was full, he was overcome by exhaustion. He barely managed to drag himself back down to the saggy cushion in his new home before passing out.

This was Randal's first underground sleeping experience, and when he opened his eyes, he didn't have a clue what time it was. How did those Mad-Rats stand it, he wondered, peering around in the dimness. Then a shiver ran down his long spine. Glinting in a corner were two shifty yellow eyes.

"Who's there?" he asked hoarsely.

"Just what I was going to ask *you*."

It sounded like no more than a pack rat. Randal got out of bed and rose to his full height. "Never mind who I am," he said, narrowing his eyes at the intruder. "Who are you?"

"One of them wharfy rats, are you?"

"I'm a wharf rat, certainly. *Yourself?*"

"Myself's Pem. Pembroke Pack-Rat."

It was the business associate of the mangy old Mad-Rat.

"Do you know the time?" Randal asked.

"Round about noon, yer honor."

Noon! If this were true, Randal had slept fifteen hours or more!

"Nice key," Pembroke commented. "Shiny."

Randal grunted.

"How is it yer not home on one of them fancy-schmancy wharves?"

"That's not really any of your business, pack rat."

"But, yer honor, business is my strong suit. Pem's got business all over the place."

"What business do you have down here?"

"Just checking my life savings." The pack rat sidled over to the stack of nickels and clinked them into a paper bag he was carrying. "I'll just get this clutter out of yer way since yer taking up residence."

"What makes you think I'm taking up residence?"

"A rat does a place up"—Pembroke gestured at the photos—"I figure he's settling in."

"Maybe I am, maybe I'm not."

"No skin off my snout either way. Be seeing you, yer honor."

Pembroke hefted his now heavy bag onto his shoulder, but as he was about to slink away, something caught his eye, and he set the bag back down. "See you brought some cash, yer honor," he said, eyeing the dollar bill.

"What about it?"

"Just, if you need to get it changed, or anything like that, I'm the rat could take care of it."

"But your life savings is only six or seven nickels."

"Saw them, did you? Well, to tell you the honest truth, yer honor, I've got a little more. Not much, but a little. Enough to change a dollar. And all I take's a nickel commission."

In fact, Pembroke could have changed many, many dollars. Uncle Moony had given him a fair wage over the years to supply him with dandelion wine and to help him with his gallery dealings—on top of which Moony had been so soused most of the time that Pembroke had been able to skim off half the cash the gallery owner gave them for the ring work. His very sizable nest egg was buried in a hundred and fifty-four different secret locations around Central Park (not counting these nickels).

"I don't need any change," said Randal.

"Well, if you think better of it, or want any business done, just give that pipe a whack with the wrench. Pem'll hear."

So saying, the pack rat picked up his bag and slouched away. As soon as he was gone, Randal stuck his dollar behind the photo of timber wolves for safe-keeping.

Pack rats aren't always reliable, but when Randal popped up to the zoo with his toothbrush and a fresh Band-Aid, he found that Pembroke had been right about the time. It *was* midday, and the zoo was packed with human beings, come to gloat over the animals they kept under lock and key.

Randal climbed to a secluded corner of the sea lions' tank, where he took his own key from around his neck and pulled the soiled Band-Aid off his tail. The sea lions were all basking in the sun on a rocky island in the middle of the tank, so Randal had the water to himself. He luxuriated in the enormous bathtub for the better part of an hour, after which he spent another forty-five minutes brushing his fur. Then he decided to visit some of his animal friends, hoping to get some sympathy for being forced out of his family crate by the newlyweds moving in next door.

He tried the Monkey House first. But the monkeys weren't very understanding. They were always grooming one another's spouses and had no idea what jealousy was. So he moved on to the North American Mammal House, home of the tightest-knit couple he knew, a pair of beavers named Buck and Bobo. Bobo was always comforting Buck, so Randal figured she might comfort him.

When he crept into their outdoor pen, the beavers were over by the splintery old telephone pole they'd been given to sharpen their teeth on.

"I must have gotten it wrong, Bobo," Buck was saying glumly as Randal crept toward them. "I always thought it was 'Take care of the little things, and the big things will take care of themselves.' But I took care of the little things—and look at us. It must be 'Take care of the big things, and the little things will take care of themselves.' I was so busy smoothing the mud on our new dam I didn't bother watching out for those human beings with their tranquilizing guns!"

"At least we *had* a dam, Buck," Bobo said brightly. "Imagine if we'd been born in captivity, like a lot of our zoo-mates. We'd never know what dams or lodges were."

"But wouldn't that be better? It's the loss that eats away at you. And to think we were on the brink of starting a family!"

"We're still young, Buck. The important thing is to keep up hope."

"Hope! Look at this thing! And look at those!"

When Randal got to the beavers, they were both staring out through their bars at a stand of tender young saplings. Unluckily for Randal, the comparison between the saplings and the splintery old telephone pole had depressed even Bobo's spirits, so he got very little comforting that day.

Nor did he get much sympathy from Mauri the elephant, whom he visited next. As usual, Mauri was lying desultorily in the shade in his outdoor pen, flicking at flies with his tail.

"Count your blessings, rat," he said. "At least you can see your mother. And you're not locked up five thousand miles from home."

Much as Randal loved the zoo, it wasn't the best-smelling place in the world, and when he got back to his new home, he wished he had some cologne to dab behind his ears. What with his photos and his toothbrush and his Band-Aids and his dollar, he'd had to leave his cologne bottle behind.

He resolved to go back to Wharf 62 to get it. This would also give him a chance to reassure his parents, for he was feeling a little bit guilty for taking off without letting them know. He would make it quick, though, and with luck he wouldn't have to set eyes on the new next-door neighbors.

He waited till evening, but when he reached Wharf 62, the day dormouse was still on duty, dozing outside the entrance crack. Randal slipped in without disturbing the puny fellow. This was usually the busiest time on the wharf, but to his surprise the place was as ratless as during the wedding. When he approached his family crate, he got another surprise. A most unpleasant one. The newlyweds' crate, crate 6, had mysteriously doubled in size!

He marched straight back to the entrance crack.

"Dormouse!" he said sharply.

"Um, oh, don't worry, I'm awake!" the dormouse cried, jerking to attention. Then he sucked in his breath. "Master Reese-Rat!"

"What's going on around here?" Randal said. "How'd crate 6 get so big?"

Instead of answering, the dormouse looked around nervously and said: "Master Reese-Rat. You came back."

"Why shouldn't I come back? Where is everybody?"

"They're, um, they're away."

"Away? All of them?"

"They're having one of their Grand Rat Chats."

"Don't tell me the human beings are raising the rent again!" Grand Rat Chats were normally called to discuss important matters like the rent.

"I, well . . . you know, Master Reese-Rat, I only work here. I don't get into politics."

"What happened to crate 6?"

"You don't know?"

"If I knew, why would I be asking? How'd it get so much bigger?"

"Well, Master Reese-Rat, first it got smaller. Then it got bigger."

"Have you been eating ratnip?"

"Me? I'm a dormouse! I never touch ratnip!"

"Crates don't grow and shrink."

"They shrink if they get burnt down."

"Burnt down?"

"In the middle of the night, they tell me. Of course, I wasn't on."

"Last night?"

"Night before."

That was the night Randal had slipped away—the newlyweds' wedding night. "Were the tenants killed?" he asked.

"They got out—just barely, I hear."

Much as Randal resented Montague and Isabel's

marriage, he wasn't sorry to hear they'd escaped. Not even they deserved to be baked to death on their wedding night. But he *was* sorry to hear that after fixing up the crate the wharf rats had decided to add a new wing for good measure. Just that Mad-Rat's dumb luck! His crate burns down and his floor space gets doubled!

"How'd the fire start, anyway?" Randal asked.

"Well, nobody's *quite* sure, Master Reese-Rat. But they have their suspicions. That's what the meeting's about."

"Why are you looking at me that way, dormouse?"

"What way is that, sir?"

"Like you just swallowed some moldy cheese."

"Well, the truth is, some of them say *you* might have been involved."

"Me!"

"They say you disappeared right after the fire started."

"And that's what the Grand Rat Chat's about?"

"Well, like I say, I just work here. But that's what I heard."

This was too much. Randal marched out of the wharf and hustled south along the edge of the West Side Highway, so angry he forgot all about his cologne.

Grand Rat Chats were held in Battery Park, at the southern tip of Manhattan, after the park closed to human beings. When Randal arrived there this evening, the park was packed with rats and the meeting was in full swing.

He slipped in among the rats on the shadowy fringes of the crowd. As at the wedding, everyone's attention was on Mr. Moberly-Rat, who was addressing them from behind a dented beer can on a park bench, the crown of his head gleaming in the light of a streetlamp. The only other rats on the bench were Randal's parents.

"And so, my fellow rats, we really have no options!" Mr. Moberly-Rat was screeching. "It would be nice if we had choices, but we don't! A crime has been committed—a violation of the laws by which we rats live.

And not just any crime. A crime that might well have turned our entire wharf, our splendid home, into an inferno from which no rat could have escaped. Thanks to the pluck and resourcefulness of two rats who will now surely have a permanent place in rat history—I refer, of course, to my daughter and son-in-law, Isabel and Montague—thanks to their intrepid firefighting, the tragedy was averted. Thanks to them, we are all here, alive and well, able to enjoy this balmy September evening. If they were present, I would ask them to step forward—but they had an engagement elsewhere."

"Too bad!" rats yelled.

"Pity!" shouted others.

"However," Mr. Moberly-Rat went on, "it was clearly not the intention of a *certain* rat that we should all be alive and well this evening. A certain rat had distinctly other plans for us. A certain rat plotted our mass destruction, starting a fire on our beloved wharf in the dead of night."

Did they think he was that "certain rat," Randal wondered, growing more livid by the second. And now Izzy and the upstart were bigger heroes than ever! He started shouldering his way through the crowd, intent on climbing the bench and setting the record straight, when a jolt of intense pain went through him. In fact, he nearly fainted. Someone had stepped on his Band-Aid—right on his injured tail!

Mr. Moberly-Rat's tail, meanwhile, twitched to the right, toward Randal's father. "It is with a mixture of sorrow and respect," he said, "that I now yield the floor to one of our greatest patriots, a real ratriot if ever there was one, my friend and colleague, Clarence Reese-Rat!"

At Grand Rat Chats, Randal's father was usually greeted by a warm ovation, but as he took over the beer can this evening, the smattering of applause was drowned out by hisses.

"I can't blame you for your cool reception, my friends," Mr. Reese-Rat said in a far hollower voice than usual. "I've always been very proud of my family name. It was handed down to me by my father, Gregory Reese-Rat, often called Gregory the Great. But they say pride comes before a rat-fall, and I'm saddened and mortified to say that my son has tarnished our name forever. I didn't want to believe it at first, but there can be no doubting it now. It's been proven beyond a shadow of a doubt that Randal fled the wharf just after the fire was set. And now he's vanished into thin air."

Woozy as Randal was with pain, his father's words penetrated his brain and he shrieked in protest. But what with his indifferent vocal cords and his weakened state, the shriek wouldn't have been loud enough to reach the rats in front even if his mother hadn't let out a heartrending wail at the same time. The rats in the back of the crowd turned on him and cried: "Ssshhhh!"

"Besides which," Mr. Reese-Rat went on, leaning heavily on the dented can, "my son was attached to

Isabel Moberly-Rat, who that very day was married to another rat—the magnificent Montague Mad-Rat. So Randal had motive. He also had opportunity, for our crate is right next door to crate 6. Motive, opportunity, fleeing the scene of the crime. And not returning."

This was intolerable. Not only being falsely accused, but having it announced to all ratdom that Isabel had picked the upstart over him! But again Randal's cry of protest was feeble, and again it coincided with a tragic wail from his mother.

"There are crimes and there are crimes," Mr. Reese-Rat went on mournfully. "But on a wharf full of wooden crates there can be no crime more terrible than arson. The firebug is the lowest form of rat life. And though it breaks my heart to say it, I have no choice but to own up that my son endangered all of us." Mr. Reese-Rat wiped a paw across his eyes. "He's my only son. But even so, I have to call on you to ferret him out of his hiding place, wherever it may be, and bring him to justice. The rathunt must begin right away. If an arsonist strikes once, he usually strikes again, and that isn't a risk we can afford to take. All I ask is that, if you find him, you bring him back alive. I beg of you not to let the mob spirit take hold. Don't tear my poor, misguided son limb from limb."

"But it wasn't me!" Randal managed to cry out.

This was heard by the rats in his vicinity.

"You're Reese-Rat's son?" demanded a stout he-rat with fiery eyes.

"It's you?" asked another—a tall she-rat carrying a sharp-looking walking stick.

Randal wanted to yell out, "Yes, and I'm innocent as the day I was born!" But the combination of the rats' menacing looks and the dreadful pain in his tail cowed him.

"Yes, I'm—well, I'm . . . I know him. I know for a fact he never plays with matches."

"Do you know where we can get our paws on him?" asked a he-rat with bulging shoulder muscles and a tail that looked like a horsewhip.

"Um, I haven't seen him just lately," Randal said.

"Shhhh!" cried an elderly rat as Randal's father cleared his throat to continue.

"But it will be best for all of us," Mr. Reese Rat said, sniffling, "if he is brought to trial. That way we can learn the whys and wherefores of his treachery, which might help us prevent such horrors in the future. And so, fellow rats, it is with a heavy heart that I ask you to . . ."

This was the last Randal heard. He felt so wretched—a mixture of pain, indignation, frustration, and plain old fear—that he just wanted to disappear into the night. So he weaved woozily out of the crowd and did exactly that.

And it was a good thing, too. For although Randal didn't hear it, the end of his father's speech included the following description: "Many of you have seen Randal out and about, but for those that haven't, he has a green splotch on his tail, which he tends to cover up with a Band-Aid. He also tends to wear a key around his neck. Anyone who brings him to justice alive will receive a ten-dollar reward from me."

Montague and Isabel were not in Battery Park because, as Mr. Moberly-Rat had told the crowd, they had "an engagement elsewhere."

They'd devoted the day before to working with the other wharf rats on the repair and enlargement of their crate: a red-letter day for Montague, who'd never seen rats who could handle hammers and nails. The work had nearly been finished, but the crate was still a bit of a construction site, so it was decided that he and Isabel should spend the night in her old room in crate 11. At sundown Montague walked his cousin Maggie, who'd used that room the night before, back to his former home. He carried her harmonica, and as they walked along underground, the cousins got to know each other.

When they stopped for a rest, she took the harmonica off his paws and, lifting it to her snout, played a few bars of one of the tunes she'd played at the reception. The echo in the storm sewer was terrific, so when she stopped playing, the tune kept bouncing around them. As they walked on, she sang a new verse:

> *Up the river Niger,*
> *Much humidity,*
> *Wearing winter fur is*
> *Big stupidity.*

This made Montague laugh. "Your songs are funny," he said. "Where'd you learn them?"

"Oh, I just make them up. I love making up songs."

When they reached the Mad-Rats' sewer pipe, it was as noisy and smoky as usual. Mrs. Mad-Rat was hat-making, Mr. Mad-Rat was castle building, and the ratlings were pestering poor Aunt Elizabeth, who was sitting on her cigarette box with a haunted look on her face.

She perked up at the sight of Maggie. "I was afraid you'd never get back!" she said.

"Monty and Izzy's crate nearly burned down last night," Maggie explained.

"What, Monty, were you melting down dyes?" Mrs. Mad-Rat asked, looking up from her work.

"No, it was arson," Montague said.

"What's arson?" chirped a ratling.

"It means some rat set the fire," said Aunt Elizabeth. "Is Isabel all right?"

"She's fine. She saved us."

"You hear that, dear?" Mrs. Mad-Rat shouted up the slope. "Monty was nearly cremated on his wedding night!"

At this news Mr. Mad-Rat spanked the mud off his paws and lumbered down off the slope. "Who's responsible, son?" he asked.

"We're not exactly sure, Dad."

"We spent the day rebuilding," said Maggie. "It was kind of fun, actually. I worked with bamboo once, but never with boards before. Some of those wharf rats are real carpenters."

"You must be starved," Mrs. Mad-Rat said with a sigh. "I suppose I should put this hat aside till tomorrow and make us a bite."

"I'll cook, Aunt," said Maggie.

"Oh, would you, dear?" Mrs. Mad-Rat said, relieved. "That's so sweet."

"Is that a wedding present, Aunt Elizabeth?" Montague asked, eyeing a seashell leaning by his bed.

"Yes," Aunt Elizabeth said.

"It's a beauty."

"I found it on a beach in Dakar," she said. "Quite a lovely beach, too."

"You're getting antsy to take off again, aren't you?"

"To be honest, Monty, I am feeling hemmed in."

"There must be some cruises coming up."

"Mm, but the next ship for Dakar isn't for three days."

"You don't want to go back to Africa, Mother," said

Maggie. "You were just there. It would bore you to tears."

"But I have to take you home."

"For heaven's sake, I'm a grown rat. I can take the ship by myself."

"Are you *sure*, dear? I did hear the *Princess Ratziwill* leaves for Montserrat tomorrow afternoon. I've never been to Montserrat—and I've always liked the sound of it. Montser*rat*."

"I'll see you off," said Maggie.

"So will I," said Montague. "Izzy'll want to come, too."

Mrs. Mad-Rat cleared her throat. "Monty, dear?"

Montague smiled. "I suppose you need supplies, Mom?"

"Well, dear, I know what an important rat you've turned into lately, married and famous and all that. But I am down to just three feathers, and my dye vats . . ."

And so it was that Montague and Isabel—and Maggie, too—missed the Grand Rat Chat. The three of them spent that morning helping put the finishing touches on crate 6, then they went to see Aunt Elizabeth off. The cruise ship was hours late disembarking—human delay, not rat—and at the last minute, after Montague and Isabel kissed Elizabeth good-bye, the traveler had second thoughts about trotting up the gangplank. On the one paw, she was dying to be on the move, out on the high seas with the wind in her fur, but, on the other paw, she suddenly found it hard to part from her daughter.

"It's been wonderful, being with you," she said. "Even when we had to share that cage with the warthog."

"It's been wonderful for me, too," said Maggie.

Seeing the tears in the mother's and daughter's eyes, Montague and Isabel backed away to give them a moment to themselves.

"I wish you'd come with me, Maggie," said Elizabeth. "Wouldn't it be fun to see more of the world?"

"I suppose. But thanks to the fire and everything, I haven't visited my father's grave yet. And afterward I really have to be getting home."

"I suppose I *could* stay another two days and sail back to Africa," Elizabeth mused.

But when the ship's horn tooted and sailors manned the crank that lifted the gangplank, her nature got the better of her. She wiped her eyes, checked her reflection in her daughter's harmonica, and kissed her on both sides of the snout—a habit she'd picked up on her travels. Then she grabbed her cigarette box and ran for the gangplank.

"What's the nicest time in Senegal?" she called down as the gangplank began to rise.

"A lot of the animals like December," Maggie said. "It's a little cooler then."

"I'll come spend part of December with you!" Elizabeth cried.

"Promise?"

"Promise!"

Maggie joined Montague and Isabel, and the three young rats stood waving on the dock till the great ship had steamed out of New York Harbor. By then the sun was quite low.

"Is it too late to go to this park?" Maggie asked.

"No, but we better hurry," said Montague. "Mom's expecting supplies."

It was nearly twilight when the three of them scampered into Central Park. Before heading for the birds' preening grounds, the best place to collect feathers for Mrs. Mad-Rat's hatmaking, Montague led the way to the laurel bush on the bank of the reservoir.

"This is where your father's buried, Maggie," Montague said. "I wish you could have known him."

"Me, too," Maggie said.

"He was a wonderful singer," said Isabel. "Maybe you could sing him one of your African songs."

Crouching there on her stranger-father's grave, Maggie lifted her harmonica and played a song in his honor. It was less jazzy, more soulful, than the ones she'd played at the reception, and when she set down her harmonica, there was no echo, so she had to sing unaccompanied.

> *To the hills high above the savanna*
> *Trudge elephants when they grow old—*
> *Slower and slower, their feet growing heavy,*
> *Their hearts, heavy too, growing cold.*
>
> *Up to a field that no one has seen—*
> *Only them, in their elephant sorrow:*
> *A gloomy old jumble of ivory and bones*
> *In the foothills of Kilimanjaro.*

Montague and Isabel exchanged a shiny-eyed look. Uncle Moony hadn't been a stranger to them—he was the rat most responsible for their happiness—and as Maggie's song drifted out across the breeze-wrinkled face of the reservoir, they thought how much they missed him.

When Maggie stopped singing, Isabel took her by the paw. "He would have loved that," she said.

"He really would have," said Montague.

"Thanks," Maggie said.

As the three rats hunched together on the water's edge, the sun set, and the reservoir darkened. Montague decided it was too late for collecting feathers and berries.

"Then I guess we better be heading home," Isabel said.

"Um, Maggie," Montague said. "What do you say you come and stay the night with us on the wharf tonight?"

"But it's your first night in your newmade crate, Monty."

"But the thing is, if we show up in the sewer empty-pawed, Mom'll go into a tailspin."

"You don't have to come, I can find my way there on my own."

"I couldn't let you."

"Come stay over with us, Maggie, it'll be fun," said Isabel. "I wish you'd stay forever. Do you have to go back on that ship day after tomorrow? You could have the new wing all to yourself."

"Good idea!" Montague said. "I've got tons of little brothers and sisters, but you're my only cousin."

"That's really nice of you," Maggie said. "But New York City . . . I admit, this park's not so bad. But the rest—I'm just not used to all the concrete and stone. And I miss home."

"Elephants and juju birds?" Montague said.

She nodded.

"You know, Izzy," Montague said, "I have an idea."

"What?" said Isabel.

"See all the stars? No way is it going to rain. We could spend the night right here, like that other time. I'll collect Mom's stuff in the morning." He twined his tail in hers and turned to his cousin. "And, Maggie, we'll give you a nice surprise tomorrow."

"It is pretty here," Maggie said. "And to tell you the truth, I wouldn't mind spending more time with my father."

So it was settled. The three of them would spend the night right there under the laurel bush.

While they were perched on Moony's grave in Central Park, Randal was trying to make it back to Moony's old forge from the Grand Rat Chat in Battery Park. But he didn't know his way around underground as well as Montague, besides which, he was still dizzy from having his tail wound stepped on and in shock from hearing his father accuse him of attempted murder. He got totally lost.

When Randal poked his head up out of a grating to get his bearings, he saw an enormous tire rolling right for him and pulled his head in like a turtle. Shuddering, he peered up through the grate at the bottom of a city bus. Another split second and he would have been rat paste.

As the bus roared away, a black cloud of exhaust shot down through the grate, coating him with soot.

"Blech!" he cried, shaking himself.

Very gingerly, he poked his head up again. There wasn't a tire within twenty rat lengths, but standing on the curbstone over the grating was a pack of rats he'd never seen before.

"There he is!" one of them cried.

"Get him!" screamed another.

Him? How did they know who he was?

But he didn't dwell on the question, for the rats were after him in a flash. Thus began the filthiest and most exhausting two hours of Randal's life.

Aboveground, he covered over five miles, all at a full sprint. He splashed through a dozen puddles, three oily. His fur collected two wads of discarded bubble gum (on sidewalks), a sprinkling of sawdust (in a greengrocer's), and a drop of soy sauce (in Chinatown). His left front paw got badly singed by a just-dropped cigarette. Worse, his left rear paw landed right where some poorly bred dog had just done his business (making

Randal think maybe they deserved to be turned into hot dogs after all).

Underground was no better. Randal covered six subterranean miles, the last in an actual working sewer! Only there, in that disgustingly smelly pipe, did his pursuers finally give up the chase.

It was long after midnight before Randal finally arrived gasping at his hideout. His tail was throbbing and every muscle in his body ached. Exhausted as he was, though, he didn't collapse on the cushion. It may have been old and saggy, but it was his bed, and he couldn't soil it with his disgusting body. He collapsed in a heap on the floor.

He might well have slept twenty-four hours if his belly hadn't starting crying out for food early the next morning. He took his toothbrush in his unburnt paw and headed up a sloping drainage pipe to the grate by the foot of the sea lions' tank. Poking his head out into the sunlight, he spotted half of a hot pretzel on the ground by a vender's cart. It was just inches from the left foot of the vender himself, a mountainous human being who looked as if he ate his own pretzels by the shovelful, but Randal was so hungry he made a daredevil dash. He grabbed his booty, dragged it underneath the cart, and gobbled it up.

His hunger satisfied, he climbed up to his favorite corner of the sea lions' tank and dove right in, even though a couple of sea lions were swimming circles around the central island in that show-offy way they have. There was a slightly fishy smell to the water—the sea lions must have just been fed—but Randal was in heaven. Even his burnt paw felt better in the cool bath.

Once he'd rinsed off the oil, the soot, the sawdust, the soy sauce, and everything else, he climbed out and gave his fur a good going-over with his toothbrush. He'd forgotten to bring along a fresh Band-Aid to replace the old one, so he climbed down off the tank to head back underground. Standing on top of the grate, stick over his shoulder, was Bernie Bat-Rat.

"Thought I might find you up here, firebug," Bernie said with a menacing smile. "Are you going to come easy, or do I have to rough you up?"

Bernie's stick was considerably bigger than Randal's toothbrush, just as Bernie was considerably bigger than Randal. Randal dropped the toothbrush and ran.

At the corner of the Monkey House, he threw a look over his shoulder. Bernie, minus his stick, was only a few rat lengths behind him. Randal darted across a wide walkway, barely escaping the wheels of a baby carriage, and flung himself between two bars into a deep, dry moat. He screamed as he landed—his burnt paw took the brunt of the impact—but Bernie was right behind him, so he scrambled straight up the other side of the moat. At the top he pulled himself through another set of bars into the elephant's outdoor pen.

"Gotcha!"

Randal let out another scream. Bernie had grabbed his poor tail, right on his wound. But in a way this was lucky, for when Bernie saw he was touching the greenish splotch, he cried "Yuck!" and instinctively let go.

As usual, Mauri was dozing on his side in the shade by his water trough. Randal dashed across the dirt expanse and ran right up the elephant's side.

"Mauri, wake up!" he cried, crouching by one of the beast's gigantic ears.

"Mama?" the elephant said.

As usual, the overgrown mama's boy had been dreaming of his mother. "No, it's me, Randal!"

The elephant's nearer eye opened. "Oh, it's you."

"I need help! That rat over there wants to murder me."

Mauri slowly lifted his enormous head. Bernie was crouched in the middle of the pen, gaping at Randal and the elephant. Mauri snaked his trunk into the water trough and, using his trunk like a fire hose, sent a spray that knocked Bernie somersaulting backward into the moat.

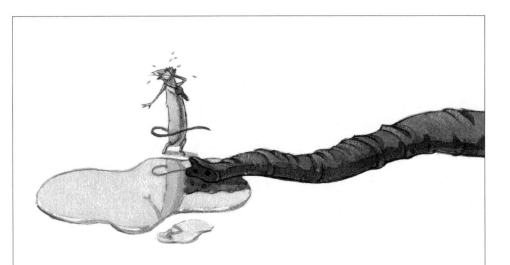

Thanks a million!" Randal cried as Bernie scampered away.

Mauri just sighed and let his head sink back down onto the ground.

"Sorry I wasn't your mother," Randal said. "I wish I could stay and chat, but I've got to make tracks."

He scurried off the elephant and dove into the pen's drainage system. In five minutes he was safe in his hideaway.

But only safe, he figured, for another twenty-four hours at most. Bernie would undoubtedly be back tomorrow with reinforcements to comb the whole zoo area.

Randal started pacing around the steam pipe, getting more and more steamed himself. What had he done to deserve being hunted like a criminal? He'd run away from home—period. And now everyone wanted to tear him limb from limb! And if he returned to the wharf and pleaded his innocence, nobody would believe him, not with all the circumstantial evidence stacked against him.

Well, one rat would believe him. The real firebug. But Randal couldn't imagine who that could be, and, of all rats, the actual culprit would be the least likely to speak up in his defense.

They would probably put him on trial. He'd never been to a trial, but his grandfather had once told him of a rat who'd stolen coins from the rent barrel and ended up being hanged by his tail from the ceiling of the wharf till he was dead as a warning to others. Hung by his tail! In public! For everyone—his parents and sister and Izzy and that upstart Mad-Rat—to point up at and shake their heads over.

He could skip town. He'd never been off Manhattan Island, though. There were bridges and tunnels that led to other places. But bridges and tunnels were notoriously dangerous, famous for rat-flattening. There were boats. But he'd never been on a boat and had no clue where they went. And he *was* a Reese-Rat. Reese-Rats had always lived here in New York City, the hub of ratdom. If he skulked away, his name would be mud.

But surely that was better than dangling from his tail till his fur rotted.

The more he thought about his plight, the angrier Randal grew. Falsely accused and falsely condemned by the whole wharf-rat community—even his family! His zoo friends never would have doomed him in such a hotheaded way. Weren't the penguins always preaching about keeping a cool head? Hadn't Mauri automatically come to his aid? Didn't the zebras warn against jumping to conclusions about creatures of any stripe? And yet his very own species had convicted him without so much as blinking! He wished he could hang all of *them* by their tails.

He stopped in front of his elephant photo and pictured Mauri plowing through Wharf 62, spearing some of the crates with his tusks, pulverizing others with his monstrous feet. That would be one way out of his fix. He could destroy all of them before they could destroy him. After all, he was innocent, while they were guilty of wrongly condemning him. He rubbed his key with his unburnt paw. He might actually be able to exchange his padlock key for the one to Mauri's cage on the zookeeper's key board. And even though Mauri was a depressed old crybaby, the chance of getting back to his mother might perk him up.

But then, even if the elephant agreed to destroy the wharf in exchange for being set free, he would never be able to get there without being seen. He was far too big to fit into any storm sewer. Human beings would spot him and recapture him and lock him up again—this time, no doubt, with a chain around one of his tree-trunk ankles.

Randal started pacing again. He was cornered—like a rat! Maybe he should bang that pipe with the wrench to call the pack rat and bribe him to bring him some matches. Then he could *really* set fire to the wharf. Though, of course, it might be hard to get past the dormouse . . .

Suddenly he stopped pacing. He was in front of another of his photos. Perhaps, he thought, fire wasn't the only way to destroy his self-proclaimed enemies. As a plan crept into his head, a smile crept over his snout.

It was then ten o'clock in the morning, and the three rats under the laurel bush were still fast asleep. What with the excitement of the wedding, and the fire, and the crate reconstruction, Isabel and Montague had been getting half their usual sleep, and what with the excitement of being on a new continent and meeting her relatives for the first time, the same was true for Maggie.

Maggie was the first of the three to wake up. As she lifted her head from her harmonica, which she'd used as a pillow, she blinked at a shimmering expanse of water and assumed she was on the banks of Lake Manantali. The laughing of hyenas had awakened her, and Lake Manantali was a favorite hyena watering place. But when she turned and saw her cousin and his young wife curled up nearby, she remembered where she was. The laughing, she realized, must be coming from human beings, not hyenas. She hadn't seen a single hyena in New York City, whereas every corner of the place seemed to be infested with people.

Hearing a loud whinny, she sat bolt upright. The whinny woke Isabel and Montague, too.

"Zebras?" Maggie whispered, excited.

"Horses," Montague said, stretching his tail. "The bridle path is right down there."

Maggie peered through the bush and saw two zebralike creatures trot by. Except they had no stripes and carried human beings on their backs.

"Gad," Isabel said, squinting at the sun. "It must be after eleven!"

"Mom'll be wringing her paws," Montague said. "I've got to get her supplies."

He whispered something in Isabel's ear.

"Great," Isabel said. "Then I'll come back and lend you a paw."

"What's going on?" Maggie asked.

"We promised you a surprise, didn't we?" Isabel said. "I'm going to show it to you."

"Shall I bring my harmonica?"

"You can leave it," Montague said, covering it up with leaves. "We'll all meet back here at around three."

Montague set off to the north, for the birds' preening grounds, and Isabel led Maggie south. At the bottom of the reservoir the two she-rats pattered along the edge of the bridle path for a while, then cut east across the Great Lawn, giving a wide berth to a group of particularly violent human beings who were smashing balls with bats. Maggie followed Isabel around a lake, through some woods, and across a bridge spanning a stream of honking yellow taxicabs. As they proceeded down a paved pathway, Maggie came to an abrupt stop.

"That's the funniest thing," she said, snout quivering.

"What?" said Isabel.

"I could have sworn I just got a whiff of lion. You don't have lions here, do you?"

Isabel smiled. "You may find New York has more to offer than you thought."

Maggie's snout quivered again—and her eyes widened. "Camel?" she said, amazed.

"Go take a look around. You'll be able to find your way back to the laurel bush, won't you?"

"Oh, sure. I have a pretty good sense of direction—and this park's a lot easier than the jungle."

"I'm going to help Monty. See you at three-ish. Have fun."

"Thanks, Isabel."

"Izzy."

"Thanks, Izzy."

Glad to give the newlyweds some time alone, Maggie continued down the pathway by herself, picking up new and interesting scents all along the way. Soon she came to a huge outdoor cage featuring a cave. Blocking the cave's mouth was a giant mass of brown fur the likes of which she'd never seen. The next cage was inhabited by a monstrous white-furred beast who, though wide awake, was equally unfamiliar. Not far from where Maggie was crouched a towering human being was telling a group of shorter (though still immense) human beings that the captive animal was something called a polar bear who normally lived near something called the Arctic Circle.

Maggie avoided the mass of humanity and scooted down the path—only to encounter a scent so overpoweringly familiar that her heart swelled with homesickness. She trailed a pair of pudgy human beings wearing shorts that exposed their oddly shaped, nearly furless legs. When one of them opened the door to a house, the scent intensified, and Maggie flung herself after them, getting in just before the door slammed shut.

It was dimmer inside than out in the sunlight, but not so dim that Maggie couldn't appreciate the astonishing sight before her: two long lines of facing cages containing every kind of ape or monkey she'd ever encountered, and more. In the first cage on her left were three black colobus monkeys; on her right, a pair of mandrills, with their terrifying red and blue faces. Baboons were shrieking, and there were chimpanzees, patas monkeys, gray-cheeked mangabeys, and gorillas. And many other kinds of monkeys she'd never laid eyes on.

It was sad, seeing them cooped up in cages instead of swinging freely through the jungle canopy. But still, the smell transported her straight home so powerfully that she couldn't help singing one of her African songs:

Up the river Niger,
Water buffalo
Not the only creature
Making progress slow.

Up the river Niger,
What a lot of fuss
When the water full of
Hippopotamus.

"How do you know about water buffalo?"

The question came from the chimpanzee's cage—but not from the chimp, who was stuffing his face with a banana. It came from a wharf rat with a Band-Aid on his tail and a key around his neck who slipped out between two bars.

"I've known water buffalo all my life," Maggie replied.

"But they don't have any here. It's one of the zoo's most glaring omissions."

"Oh. Well, I live in Africa."

"You're kidding."

Maggie shook her head. "I'm Maggie," she said, extending a paw.

"I'm, uh, my name's Gregory." Of course his name was really Randal, but that name had become infamous, so he hit on his grandfather's. "I like your song, Maggie."

"Why, thank you, Gregory. Do you like chimps, too?"

"Um, actually . . ."

"I'm wild about them."

"You are?"

"Of course. They're extremely intelligent—almost as intelligent as rats."

"You know, you're right. Most rats are too rat-centric to appreciate that. But then, I suppose, if you're from Africa, you might be different. What's it like there?"

"It's magnificent. Parts of it are getting overrun by human beings, of course, but from what Mother tells me, that's true everywhere. Mother's a globe-trotter."

"How unusual. And you've . . . you've actually seen a hippo in the wild?"

"Hordes."

"And lions?"

"Scads."

"And rhinos?"

"Well, rhinos are scarce. But I once saw a white one."

"A white rhino!"

"With a baby. But the baby wasn't white. Watch out!"

She grabbed his key and yanked him to the left, barely saving him from a hiking boot.

"Thanks," Randal said, startled. He'd been so transfixed by this she-rat that he'd actually forgotten to keep a lookout for human beings. "You saved my fur."

Maggie just smiled. "What's the key to?"

"Oh, it's only for good luck."

"Well, it worked."

He grinned. "You're right. But still, maybe we better get out of here. We can cut through the gorillas'."

The gorillas' cage had an opening to an outdoor playground featuring a tire swing. The suspended tire was as big as the one that had nearly flattened Randal yesterday. In it an overfed male gorilla was swinging lazily back and forth picking his nose and ears while human beings beyond the playground's bars made fun of him.

Randal led Maggie across to the shadowy side of the playground. When they neared the bars, he pulled her behind a rock.

"What's wrong, Gregory?"

"Shh."

"What is it?" Maggie whispered.

It was just a couple of brown rats skulking around under a park bench on the walkway outside the gorillas' playground. But even they might have heard about Randal, so it seemed best to avoid them.

"They're terrible bores," Randal said, giving one of his trademark yawns as the brown rats pattered off toward the Penguin House.

"I smell elephant," Maggie remarked as they came out between the bars.

"Oh, would you like to meet my friend Mauri? He's kind of a big baby, always crying for his mama, but I like him anyway."

"It would be a pleasure."

It turned out to be a pleasure for Mauri, too. The elephant had been born in a place called Tanzania, and while Maggie had never been there, she knew dozens of creatures that had, including a leopard named Bofu whom Mauri thought he remembered from his childhood. But in the pleasure department, Randal was the winner. He'd always felt alienated from other rats, but here was one who shared his fascination with other species! And she knew the animals in the fur, in the wild, not just from photos or in cages. What's more, she was very attractive, even exotic-looking, and had a lovely singing voice.

She was a good storyteller, too. Mauri just lay there

on his side as always, but before long, Maggie's descriptions of Africa actually got him to lift his head a bit.

"How did you end up here, Mauri?" Maggie asked him.

"Oh, that's all a long time ago."

"You've forgotten?"

"Forgotten! Never."

"How *did* you end up here?" Randal asked.

Mauri looked off at the pen's bars. A tear rolled out of one of his eyes and weaved its way down his wrinkly cheek.

"Ivory hunters," he said.

"They wanted your tusks?" said Maggie.

"My mother's. Mine were still too small. I was less than a year old."

"What happened to your mother?" Maggie asked.

A tear squeezed out of his other eye. "They shot her."

"Dead?"

"Dead."

"Your mother's dead?" Randal cried, as surprised as he was horrified. "And you were there?"

"Beside her."

"What did you do?"

"I charged them."

"You did?"

"All I wanted was to kill them—to avenge Mama. But they threw a net over me. They put me in a steaming-hot box—and I ended up here in this zoo. I've been here ever since."

"You never told me that," Randal said, chagrined at having thought of Mauri as a crybaby and a mama's boy.

"I never told anybody. But hearing about Africa . . ."

No wonder the gigantic beast always just lay there like a lump, Randal thought.

"You know, Maggie sings African songs," he said.

"You do?" Mauri said. "You wouldn't know any about elephants, would you?"

The only elephant song Maggie had ever sung was the one from last night, and a song about an elephant graveyard didn't seem a good choice for Mauri. So she made up a new one.

> *Elephant excellent memory*
> *Famous far and wide*
> *Same as long long curling trunk*
> *And thick thick elephant hide.*
>
> *Less well known is heart and courage*
> *Elephant always show*
> *On hot hot Serengeti plain,*
> *In Kilimanjaro snow.*
>
> *Like proud old Pubadingophant,*
> *Bellow in the dusk,*
> *Battling pride of angry lion,*
> *Sacrificing tusk.*

Or great Kukuwanangaphant,
Seven ton at least,
Pulverize rhinoceros
And every other beast.

South of Kisangani town,
Kimpopophant the king,
Hide is full of pygmy dart
Never feel the sting.

But word has not spread far and wide,
No one in Kenya hear,
Uganda or Rwanda or
Burundi or Zaire,

That bravest of the elephants,
True elephant patriarch,
Live not in Africa at all
But right in Central Park.

When Maggie stopped singing, Randal could hardly believe his eyes. The zookeeper with his prod was nowhere in sight, yet Mauri jerked up onto his knees and rose all the way to his feet—to his full, majestic, elephant height.

W hen he met Maggie, Randal had just finished transacting some business—business related to his survival plan—with the chimpanzee. His intention had been to do one other piece of business and spend the rest of the daylight hours lying low. He was, after all, the object of a citywide rathunt. But he was so taken with Maggie that he risked giving her a tour of the zoo.

After saying good-bye to the rejuvenated Mauri, he took her to visit the rhinoceros. The rhino was sound asleep, snoring noisily away in the dirt, but the giraffe, whom they visited next, was wide awake, and she and Maggie soon established a common African acquaintance: a gossipy jackdaw named Jeri. Keeping to the shadows, Randal took Maggie to see the gazelles next. Gazelles have no memories at all—they can barely re-

member what they had for dinner the night before—
but they are very graceful.

"That was wonderful," Maggie said after they
slipped out of the gazelles' pen. "I wish I didn't have to
leave."

"You have to leave?" Randal said.

"I've got to meet my cousin and his wife at the reservoir at three."

"But . . ." Randal had been enjoying her company so
much that he hadn't imagined their time together ending. "Do you have to go?"

"I'm afraid so. It's been fun, though."

"I . . ."

"Yes?"

"Well, I just can't get it out of my head. The song
you sang for Mauri. It's the nicest thing I ever saw anyone do."

"Oh, but he *is* a brave elephant. Imagine seeing your
mother shot and trying to do something about it, only
to end up stuck in a cage."

"Still, it was such a kind gesture on your part. And
you sang it so beautifully."

"Why, thank you. To tell you the truth, I usually do
better. It's hard without my harmonica."

"Harmonica?" Randal said, remembering the she-
rat he'd seen leaning on a harmonica up on the dumpster at Isabel and Montague's wedding.

"Mm, usually I play the tune first on my harmonica."

"Huh. May I ask your last name?"

"Mad-Rat."

"Mad-Rat!"

"Is something wrong? My cousin's quite popular—Montague Mad-Rat."

"*That's* the rat you're going to meet?"

"Him and Isabel. Do you know them?"

Randal just gaped at her.

"May I ask your last name, Gregory?"

"My last name? Sad-Rat. Gregory Sad-Rat."

"Funny. You do look sad, all of a sudden."

How could he not? He'd met a wonderful, once-in-a-lifetime rat and she'd turned out to be one of those detestable Mad-Rats, his least favorite clan in all ratdom.

"Thanks for showing me around, Gregory. I'm leaving tomorrow, so I probably won't see you again, but I'll always remember today. Bye now."

"Bye," he said quietly.

She gave him a curious look, then shrugged and pattered off to keep her appointment with the two rats he resented most in the world.

What a strange rat, Maggie thought as she cut through the tall grass bordering the lake at the foot of the Great Lawn. He'd seemed so friendly and enthusiastic—and so interested in Africa—that she'd been on the verge of suggesting he pay a visit. And then, when it came time to part, he barely bothered saying goodbye. She would have to ask Isabel and Montague if blowing hot and cold was a New York City trait.

When she got back to the laurel bush by the reservoir, Izzy and Monty were waiting for her. But Maggie didn't ask them any questions. Neither of them could have answered, for their cheeks were stuffed with berries. All in all, they looked pretty funny, what with their tails looped around bouquets of feathers.

"Aunt's going to be ecstatic," Maggie said, pulling her harmonica out from under the leaves.

Maggie was right. When they got back to the sewer

pipe, Mrs. Mad-Rat let out a whoop of such pure delight that the ratlings all stopped their whining.

"Izzy, too, such a glorious daughter-in-law!" Mrs. Mad-Rat cried as Isabel and Montague spat out their berries and dropped their feathers. "Look, a bluebird feather, I won't even have to dye it! And a cardinal feather, too!"

As Mrs. Mad-Rat sorted the feathers, she was so excited she didn't even ask them what had delayed them a day.

"Hiya, kids!" Mr. Mad-Rat called from his be-castled slope.

"Is that 108 or 109, Dad?" Montague asked.

"Still 108. Adding flying buttresses."

"It's a beauty, Uncle," said Maggie.

"It is, isn't it?" he said proudly.

"Play the music, Cousin Maggie!" cried a chorus of ratlings.

Maggie had done a lot of walking that day, and she was very tired. But since she was leaving tomorrow and her little cousins were so insistent, she played them a few songs, ending the concert with a lullaby that magically put them all to sleep.

Only then did she ask Isabel and Montague about the quirky behavior of the rat she'd met at the zoo.

"Did you get his name?" Montague asked.

"Sad-Rat. Gregory Sad-Rat."

"Never heard of him. Though of course I don't know that many rats."

"I've never heard of him either," said Isabel, who had a far wider acquaintance.

"Well, he was kind of cute," Maggie said, "and he seemed very interested in Africa. I don't think he was faking it just to be polite. But then when I told him my name . . ."

"Uh-oh," said Montague. "That used to happen to me."

"But Mad-Rat's a name of honor now!" Isabel objected. "Your new friend must live in a cave or something."

"By the way," said Mrs. Mad-Rat, looking up from the vat she was stirring. "Did Elizabeth get off all right yesterday?"

"Her ship was delayed," Montague said, "but it finally left. We're trying to talk Maggie into not leaving tomorrow."

"Oh, do stay, dear," Mrs. Mad-Rat said. "You have

such a way with the ratlings. Though Elizabeth tells me you're very popular in Africa."

"You ought to stay at least to see the leaves turn in the park," Isabel said. "It's lovely."

"I wish I could, but I'm afraid . . . not that I'm really popular, but I do have to get back."

"If you really must go," Isabel said, "we'll throw you a good-bye party tonight on the wharf."

"I don't know if your wharfy friends are in a party mood, dear," Mrs. Mad-Rat said.

"Why do you say that?"

"A pack of them stopped by an hour or two ago. Very serious, they seemed. Hunting for that firebug. Name of Reese-Rat."

A troubled look crossed Isabel's face. Though she'd missed the Grand Rat Chat, she knew Randal was the primary suspect in the case of the crate fire, but somehow she didn't like the idea of him being hunted down. For in spite of the evidence against him, she couldn't believe he'd really tried to incinerate her.

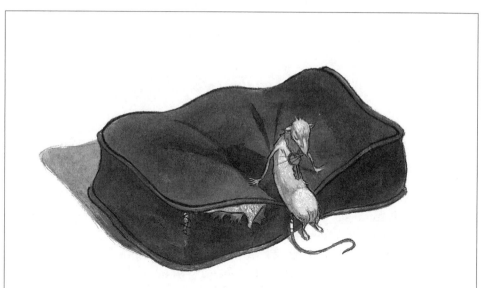

After Maggie left him, Randal did some business in the North American Mammal House and then returned to his underground hideout. He should have been a happy rat. Not only had he escaped the rathunt so far, he'd also come up with a plan for getting his revenge on the whole wharf of them. But he slumped down on the edge of the saggy cushion, depressed. For the first time in his life he'd come across a she-rat who actually shared his interests, and she turned out to be one of those unspeakable sewer dwellers!

Randal lay back on his bed with a sigh. Stuck up over the bed was his elephant photo, and from somewhere far down the pipe he heard:

> *... bravest of the elephants,*
> *True elephant patriarch,*

Live not in Africa at all
But right in Central Park.

It was only in his head, of course. Just as the memory of Mauri's smiling face, towering high up in the sky, was only in his head. But Mauri *had* smiled that way. It was the first time he'd ever seen Mauri smile at all.

Randal sat back up. The fact of the matter was, Maggie *wasn't* a sewer dweller. Unlike those other Mad-Rats, she lived in Africa. And her mother was a "globe-trotter." Maybe all Mad-Rats weren't alike. Maybe some of them weren't filthy upstarts who made things with their paws. A song, after all, was different from one of those stupid painted seashells. A song wasn't something crass that you could hold in your paws. It existed—but at the same time it didn't.

I'm leaving tomorrow, so I probably won't see you again.

Where was she going? Back to Africa?

But I'll always remember today.

Randal stood up off the bed. He, too, would always remember today. But was today to be the only time he got to spend with her?

He sank back down. She was a Mad-Rat. How could he possibly have feelings for a Mad-Rat!

Over the next few hours Randal stood up and sank back down a lot. Every time he thought of his new friend's last name, he would hear Mr. Blowhard Moberly-Rat proclaiming: "We are gathered here today to celebrate the marriage of my daughter, Isabel, to the young rat responsible for the very fact that we are . . . gathered here today"—and he would feel sick to his stomach. But every time he thought of her first name, Maggie, he would hear her singing to Mauri, and his eyes would mist over.

Finally, while nodding his head to the elephant tune, Randal picked up the crescent wrench and gave the pipe a good whack. The pack rat appeared in no time— almost as if he'd been waiting for the call.

"That was quick," Randal said.

"Time's money," said the pack rat. "How's yer honor this evening?"

This gave Randal a start. "Is it evening already?"

"Sun's set."

"The zoo's closed?"

"Yup. You wanted Pem for something?"

Randal hesitated, his eyes drifting to one of his photos. But he soon looked back at the pack rat. "You said it's your business to know where things are?"

"This what you looking fer?" Pembroke pulled a toothbrush out of his bag.

"Why, that's mine!"

"Funny. I found it lying by a bench up in the zoo."

"I dropped it."

"Pity."

"Look, pack rat. Do you know where the Mad-Rats live? It's some sewer or other."

"The ones that go in for hats and mud castles?"

"Sounds right."

"I've been by there."

"Could you take me?"

"It could be arranged. Fer a price."

"How much?"

"When do you want to go?"

Randal made a quick calculation in his head. "In three hours," he said.

"On the dot, is it? If it's any old time, it's a quarter, but if it's by appointment, it's fifty."

"Fifty cents! That's outrageous."

"Things is inflated these days, yer honor. Ever since them shell paintings went so high."

"But fifty cents, just to show me a sewer!"

"Tell you what. I'll toss in the toothbrush. Can't be fairer than that."

Randal sighed. His revenge plan called for a lot of running around in the next three hours, and the idea of giving his fur a good brushing before seeing Maggie again appealed to him deeply. "Could you throw in some cologne?" he asked.

"Fresh out, yer honor."

"Well, you're fleecing me . . . but I guess I have no choice."

"Wait here. I'll get yer change."

"I'll pay you when we get there."

"Pem always gets paid in advance."

"Not at these prices he doesn't."

Pembroke could tell by Randal's tone of voice that he

wasn't going to win this argument, so he shrugged and said: "Meet you here in three hours?"

"Which is closer to the Mad-Rats', here or Wharf 62?"

"Why?"

"I could meet you either place."

The truth was, Pembroke had been fudging a bit when he said he knew where the Mad-Rats lived. Though old Moony had described the place to him, the pack rat didn't know the exact location. But he knew from experience that when it comes to parting rats from their money, the best policy is to act sure of yourself—like general ratitioners when they tell you what's ailing you. "It's about the same," he said. "Take yer pick."

"Wharf 62 then."

"Inside or out?"

"Outside! The north corner. And make sure you don't draw attention to yourself around there."

"Hush-hush, is it? If it's hush-hush, it's an extra dime."

"Listen, pack rat, if there's any extra dime in this deal, it's the one that's going to get shoved down your throat."

Pembroke backed up a step. "No need fer violence, yer honor, no need fer violence. Pem'll be there in three hours."

"Outside Wharf 62."

"Outside Wharf 62."

Inside Wharf 62, Isabel was calling on Digby Dinner-Rat. She was pleading with him to make his ratatouille for Maggie's good-bye party. It was Isabel's first time ever inside crate 44, the great chef's home. Except for a cushion in a corner, the entire place was one big kitchen. There was a good-sized hole in the ceiling so that, when Digby cooked, the smoke could escape.

"I'm afraid it's impossible," he said. "Too short notice."

"Oh, but *please*, Mr. Dinner-Rat. It's Maggie's last night in New York."

"I'm afraid making ratatouille isn't quite like slicing off a piece of Swiss cheese, Miss Moberly-Rat—er—Mrs. Mad-Rat."

"I *know* that, Mr. Dinner-Rat. But if you set your

mind to it, I'm sure you could pull it off. We want to put our best paw forward for the send-off—and there's nothing on earth like your ratatouille."

"Even if I wanted to, I don't have enough ingredients."

"Are there any leftovers from the other night?"

Digby frowned. Usually his food was so popular there wasn't a nibble left over. But at the wedding feast, rats had jumped up to dance to that grating music instead of begging for seconds.

"Actually, there are some," he said sourly. "I overestimated a bit."

"Couldn't you just spice them up a little?"

"Spice them up! Everything was seasoned perfectly the first time!"

"I didn't mean it that way. I meant—add to it a little." Isabel batted her beady eyes at him. "Won't you, Mr. Dinner-Rat, as a personal favor?"

"Well . . ."

"Hooray!"

"But . . ."

"But what? Just name it."

But that rude stranger-rat better not start in with her harmonica in the middle of dinner was what Digby wanted to say. However, the harmonica was a dangerous subject, so all he said was: "But it'll take a couple of hours."

"Of course it will! That's perfect. Everyone's tired from the rathunt. It'll give them time for naps."

After leaving crate 44, Isabel made the rounds of the wharf, issuing party invitations. Once she'd asked everyone, she returned to the fabulously made-over crate 6, where she and Montague caught a few winks in their bedroom while Maggie napped in the new wing.

Eventually, the smell of ratatouille filled the wharf, and hundreds of napping rats woke up, sniffing. They quickly assembled out in the main aisle, but Digby, world-class chef that he was, kept them waiting quite a while before serving up his masterpiece.

When he finally did, he was most gratified, for the rats had worked up big appetites rathunting and dug in with a vengeance. But once again Maggie ate only a mouthful, and Ellie, noticing that the musical foreigner wasn't eating, asked if she would play the jujubird song. Maggie picked up her harmonica and obliged—whereupon Ellie pulled Bernie Bat-Rat away from his dinner to dance with her.

"You'd think Ellie would keep a low profile, under the circumstances," an older she-rat whispered to her husband.

"Mm, with a firebug brother," her husband agreed.

But most rats were too swept away by the beat to notice such niceties. Somebody cried out for the Congo song, and Maggie played that one, too. By the end of it nearly all the younger rats were dancing away.

"Another!" they cried.

"We'll make you a stage!" said Bernie.

In no time he and his pals built a little stage out of the scrap lumber left over from the crate 6 renovations. Maggie climbed onto it and struck up another jazzy tune.

Not even Isabel could resist this one. "Come on, Monty," she said, tugging him away from his meal.

Montague, not being a polished dancer, didn't twirl Isabel around the way Bernie was twirling Ellie. But much as Isabel loved to spin, she enjoyed swaying calmly in Montague's paws, her snout resting on his shoulder. That way everything wasn't a blur, and she could enjoy the sight of the others enjoying themselves.

One rat who clearly wasn't having fun was Digby Dinner-Rat. A few minutes ago he'd been happily watching the ravenous rats from the doorway to crate 44, but now that his ratatouille had been abandoned, the look on his face was far from pleased.

"Excuse me a minute, Monty," said Isabel, breaking away. "Mr. Dinner-Rat looks a little put out."

She decided she would ask Digby to dance. But by

the time she got to crate 44, he'd gone inside. The door was open. She stepped into the huge kitchen and saw the great chef standing with his back to her, staring into a pot. Only then did it occur to her that he probably wasn't a fan of dancing, having only one hind leg.

Before she could think what to say, Digby started talking to himself. "Idiot! It's mostly metal. How could you think it would burn? Fool! If you'd used your head, this would never have happened. You could have just thrown the lousy thing in the river!"

At that same moment Randal was staring down at the very river Digby Dinner-Rat had in mind. Crouched on the northern side of Wharf 62, Randal was watching the moonlit waters lap against the pilings that held the wharf up. But the only river he could hear was the river of cars and trucks on the West Side Highway.

Every now and then, a nearby traffic light turned red, and there was a brief break in the traffic. During one such break, Pembroke Pack-Rat scuttled across the highway. As he crept over to the north end of the wharf, hitching his bag up his back, he noted that Randal had brought along his toothbrush and that, wrapped tightly around the handle, secured by a rubber band, was a nice green dollar bill. A momentary glint of the same green flashed in Pembroke's yellowish eyes.

"Three hours on the snout, yer honor," he said, sidling up to Randal.

Randal looked over his shoulder with a scowl. "Sshh! There's a night dormouse."

"Sorry," Pembroke said, dropping his voice.

"Ready to take me to the Mad-Rats', pack rat?"

"Pem's at yer service."

Pembroke led the way to the nearest grating and popped down into a storm sewer.

"You can hand that down, yer honor," he said, peering back up. "I can carry it in my bag, if you want."

However, Randal managed to climb down without giving up his toothbrush. "Which way?" he said.

"Just keep on my tail, yer honor."

In the three hours since their last meeting, Pembroke had made a tour of the sewers and located the Mad-Rats' home. He took a loopy route, so if the customer wanted to make a repeat visit he'd have to rehire him, but they eventually arrived.

"That's it, just up this pipe."

"Good grief," Randal said, squinting through the smoke at the astonishing array of feather hats and mud castles. "It's even worse than I imagined."

"It is a little thick in here. Think I'll be going—unless you need something else."

Pembroke set down his bag and pulled out two quarters. He'd unearthed them from one of his hundred-and-fifty-four secret hiding places in Central Park, a hole three rat lengths from the base of one of the statues human beings erect to honor themselves. Randal pulled the rubber band from his toothbrush, unrolled the dollar bill, and exchanged it for the fifty cents.

"A brush and two quarters," Pembroke commented. "What you need is a bag, yer honor."

"That's true," Randal said.

"You can have mine fer a quarter."

"Get out of here, pack rat!"

Pembroke stuffed the dollar into his bag with a shrug and did as he was told.

Left alone, Randal gave his fur a brushing, then set the toothbrush beside what remained of his fortune and crept empty-pawed down the sewer pipe. With every step the smoke grew denser and the screeches of ratlings louder. But neither the smoke nor the racket seemed to be bothering a matronly she-rat who was dipping feathers in a vat.

"Excuse me," Randal said, walking up to her. "Aren't you Mrs. Mad-Rat?"

"Don't know a thing about him," she replied, not even lifting her eyes from her work.

"Who are you talking about?"

"The firebug. Some of your wharfy friends already asked."

"Firebug? Who said anything about a firebug? I'm looking for Maggie Mad-Rat."

At this Mrs. Mad-Rat glanced up from the vat. "You know Maggie?"

Randal nodded. "Isn't she staying here with you?"

"She was."

"She hasn't gone back to Africa already, has she?"

"Leaves first thing in the morning. But tonight there's a going-away party for her on that big wharf." Mrs. Mad-Rat sighed. "I *wanted* to go, of course. But unfortunately my fires are at *just* the perfect dyeing temperature. Mr. Mad-Rat would have gone, too"—she cocked her head at a muddy he-rat working away on the crazy slope of castles—"if he wasn't putting the *last* finishing touches on 108."

"After the party Maggie's coming back here?" Randal asked.

"No, we said our farewells and bon voyages. She's spending the night with my son and his wife. They're going to see her off in the morning."

"She's spending the night on Wharf 62?"

"I believe that's the one."

Mrs. Mad-Rat returned to her feather dyeing. So she didn't notice the color drain out of Randal's ears, or the zombie-like way he crept off down the smoky pipe.

By the time Maggie had played a dozen tunes, the harmonica was growing heavy in her paws. She hated disappointing the wharf rats, who clamored for more after every number, but at last she had to stop.

"I'm afraid I need to get some sleep," she said. "My boat leaves early in the morning."

"Boat schmoat!" a rat cried.

"Yeah, stick around!" cried another.

"You could be a star!" cried Bernie.

"New York's the big time!" added one of his pals.

"Thank you, I do love it here," Maggie said. "But I really can't stay."

"Play one more for the road then," Ellie shouted.

"I would, but I can barely pick up my harmonica anymore."

"Sing us one then!" a rat suggested. "You haven't sung all night."

"Yeah, sing us one!" cried others.

So Maggie sang one:

> *On the river Congo,*
> *On the river Nile,*
> *On the river Niger,*
> *Full of crocodile,*
>
> *Many bird is hidden,*
> *Serpent wear disguise,*
> *But everything familiar,*
> *Never big surprise.*
>
> *On the river Hudson,*
> *Everything so strange!*
> *Sunset blocked by buildings*
> *Big as mountain range!*

Instead of dancing, the wharf rats crowded close to the little stage so as not to miss a word. Even the night dormouse was lured over. He usually kept his dealings with rats on a strictly business basis, but this one's whimsical music infected even him.

Nor was the audience confined to the wharf.

After leaving Mrs. Mad-Rat, Randal headed back to Wharf 62 in a daze. The news that Maggie was spending the night there threw him into such a quandary that he totally forgot his toothbrush and fifty cents. The truth was, he almost wished he'd never run into her outside the chimpanzee's cage.

When he'd heard Maggie singing that first time, he'd just struck a deal with the chimp. It was part of his survival/revenge plan. After giving up on the idea of Mauri destroying his wharf-rat enemies, he'd stopped in front of his photo of beavers gnawing tree trunks, and as he'd stared at it, the tree trunks had magically turned into the pilings that held up Wharf 62. It had come to him: If the beavers gnawed through all the pilings, the wharf would collapse into the river. No doubt few, if any, of the tenants would drown—the rats would desert the wharf like a sinking ship—but in the chaos afterward they would surely forget about the rathunt. And if his family's crate had to be sacrificed along with the others, that was a small price to pay for such a perfect rataliation.

Inspired by his brainstorm, Randal had hustled straight up to the zoo to pay his beaver friends a visit. They were just as he'd last seen them: staring out longingly through the bars of their outdoor pen at the tender young saplings beyond their reach.

"I always thought it was 'All things come to the beaver who waits,'" Buck was saying to Bobo. "But it must be—"

"Oh, Buck," said Bobo. "You shouldn't talk like that."

"Why not?"

"Because . . . because . . ."

Randal tapped their flat tails. "Because you never know when things might look up," he said.

"Rat!" said Buck, turning.

"What do you mean?" said Bobo.

"I mean you might be able to get out of here."

The beavers' eyes widened.

"I've been thinking about it," Randal said. "It could happen."

"How?" said Bobo.

"You could waltz right out the door."

"But it's locked," said Buck. "And the zookeeper keeps all the keys on that big ring he carries around."

"There's duplicates on the key board in his office," said Randal.

"But if you take a key off the key board, he'll notice."

"Not if I replace it with this," Randal said, touching the key around his neck. "Of course, we'd have to wait till the zoo closes."

"But how could we turn the key in the lock?" Buck said. "Excuse me for saying so, but you're way too small to reach it. And even if our paws could fit through, they're made for swimming and dam building, not turning keys."

"Oh, but there must be a way!" Bobo cried.

"Don't count on it," said Buck. "I used to think it was 'Where there's a will, there's a way,' but I've found out it's 'Where there's a will, there's a won't.'"

"I wouldn't be so sure of that," Randal said.

"You have an idea?" said Bobo.

"I might. I'm not going to tell you, in case it doesn't work out, but be ready to go at nightfall."

"What a wonderful rat!" Bobo said.

"Why would you go to all this trouble for us?" Buck said doubtfully.

"Well," said Randal, "I was hoping you might do me one little favor in return."

"Anything!" Bobo cried.

Randal described Wharf 62 and the pilings that held it up. "There must be a dozen or more. And they're pretty thick."

"They sound delicious," said Bobo. "They're really in a river?"

"The Hudson," said Randal.

"The Hudson! Do you hear that, Buck? I've heard its headwaters are in a lovely wilderness."

"But even if we could escape the zoo," Buck said, "how would we get to this wharf without being recaptured?"

"Underground," said Randal. "There's a missing manhole cover where some human beings are working on Fifth Avenue. You could fit through. I know the way from there. Could you gnaw through a dozen pilings in one night?"

"With pleasure," said Bobo.

"Well, we could try, anyway," Buck said, more realistically. "Though if we do get through them all, the wharf you're talking about will fall into the water."

"It's rotten to the core," Randal said. "Better it should go all at once than crumble little by little."

"When we're done, we can swim upstream?" Bobo asked.

"Absolutely," said Randal. "See you in a few hours."

From there he'd gone straight to the Monkey House. The chimpanzee, he knew, was tall enough to reach the lock on the beavers' cage and had human-like fingers that could easily turn a key. Randal figured he could exchange his key for the chimp's first and set the chimp free in exchange for his help with the beavers' lock.

But, unlike the beavers, the chimp showed no interest at all in being set free.

"What would I do out in this city, rat? There's no

jungle. The cabdrivers are madmen. In the winter I'd freeze my tail off. At least the zoo's heated, and they feed you."

"After you help me get the beavers out, you could just come back here."

"What's in it for me then?"

They really were nearly as smart as rats, these chimps. But Randal finally won him over by promising to steal him an extra banana from the zoo's commissary every day for a month. He'd just delivered the first one, in fact, when he heard Maggie singing and inquired about her knowledge of water buffalo.

After making his arrangement to meet the pack rat at Wharf 62, Randal had gone up to the zoo and slipped into the zookeeper's office through a heating duct. It was a cinch to get the key to the chimpanzee's cage from the key board and replace it with his own, but when he delivered the key to the chimp, the crazy primate nearly gave him a heart attack by popping it into his mouth as if it were a piece of cheese. The chimp was only fooling around, though. He soon spat the key out and used it to let himself out.

This caused such a sensation in the Monkey House that Randal was afraid the rumpus would attract the night watchman. But the chimp calmed his fellow primates down by promising to be back in a few minutes. Meanwhile Randal had to dash back to the office and exchange the key to the chimp's cage for the Monkey House key. And once he and the chimp were outside,

he had to dash back and exchange the Monkey House key for the North American Mammal House key. And once they were inside the Mammal House, he had to dash back and exchange that key for the key to the beavers' cage. And once the beavers were out, he had to make all those same dashes in reverse. It was an hour and a half before the chimp was back in his cage and Randal was finally able to lead the beavers through the shadowy zoo, up the stairs to Fifth Avenue, and down the open manhole.

The beavers were so thrilled to be free that they didn't mind the underground journey a bit, even though it was slow going and their fur got filthy squeezing through some of the tighter spots in the storm sewers and drainage pipes. But they hit a snag when they finally arrived at the waterfront. Neither beaver could squeeze up through any of the holes in the storm-sewer grating. Nor could they locate any open manholes in the area.

"We'll just have to go back," Buck said with a sigh. "For a minute there I was thinking it was 'All bad things come to an end.' But it must be good things."

Bobo wasn't so easily discouraged. When they found a closed manhole cover, she climbed onto Buck's back and managed to dislodge it. The three of them popped up through the hole onto a cobblestone side street just off the West Side Highway.

"Look, Buck!" Bobo cried. "Not a bar in sight!"

"Not a tree or stream either," Buck grumbled.

But not even Buck could contain himself when Randal led them across the highway to the north end of Wharf 62. Stretched out before them like a giant snake, scales shimmering in the moonlight, was the Hudson River. Buck gave Bobo a joyous hug, then dove right in. Bobo plopped giddily in after him.

Watching from above, Randal suddenly realized that there was nothing to stop the beavers from swimming straight upstream to their beloved wilderness. But beavers are as dependable as they are industrious, and, sure enough, they both looked up and waved as soon as they surfaced.

"This water's polluted, rat!" Buck cried.

"Gosh, I'm sorry!" Randal called down. "I didn't know. Is it going to hurt you?"

"We can make it till morning," said Bobo. "Are those the pilings over there?"

"That's right," Randal said.

"There's way too many," said Buck.

"But we can try," said Bobo. "We'll start with these ones nearest shore and work our way out."

"Great!" Randal cried. "Thanks a million, you guys!"

"No, thank you a million, rat!" cried Bobo.

Randal had been watching the beavers at work when the pack rat arrived to take him to the Mad-Rats' sewer. Though there were an awful lot of pilings to be gnawed through, the beavers were working like creatures possessed, fired by dreams of freedom, and Randal could just picture the wharf crumbling and all the crates, odd- and even-numbered alike, floating gloriously out to sea. Just what the rats all deserved for unfairly condemning him!

But if the wharf collapsed, it was possible that some rat or other might get knocked on the head and drown. He wouldn't have minded a bit if this happened to Bernie Bat-Rat. But once he found out that Maggie was going to be spending the night there, his perfect revenge seemed less than perfect.

It took a long time, but he finally found his way back to Wharf 62 from the Mad-Rats'. The entrance crack, he saw, was unattended. Creeping up to it, he heard faint singing. Just visible above a pack of rats was Maggie's head, and by cupping his ears with his paws, Randal could make out her lyrics:

> *Here in New York City,*
> *Everything bizarre;*
> *Nothing like Mombasa,*
> *Nothing like Dakar.*
>
> *Many dollar needed*
> *Just to pay the rent,*
> *Many screeching tire,*
> *Many accident.*
>
> *But city rat is gracious*
> *On Wharf 62,*

Isabel and Monty,
Lavinia and Hugh.

Also down in sewer
And up on avenue,
Rat is very friendly,
Even in the zoo.

Thank you, everyone,
For hospitality;
Almost wish I wasn't
Heading out to sea.

But being somewhere different,
Hardest thing for rat,
Happiest at home in
Ratty habitat . . .

The song cast a spell on Randal. Even after it was over, it echoed in his head:

Rat is very friendly,
Even in the zoo . . .

Repeating Maggie's lyrics to himself, Randal returned to the Mad-Rats' sewer pipe, where he was pleased to see that the pack rat hadn't come back and filched his last two quarters. Randal picked up the coins but, with a pang of regret, left his toothbrush.

Even without the toothbrush, the trip back to his hideout under the zoo was a long haul. Thanks to the coins, he had to walk the whole way on his hind legs, and he was so bleary-eyed from his day of dashing around the zoo and journeying to the wharf that he took two wrong turns. It was midnight when he finally arrived at the forge. But again he didn't collapse on the saggy cushion. He dumped the quarters, picked up the crescent wrench, and banged the pipe.

Late as it was, the pack rat appeared almost instantly. "Looking a little ragged, yer honor," Pembroke commented, dumping his bag.

Normally this would have thrown Randal into a tizzy. But he just said: "How'd you like to earn another fifty cents, pack rat?"

"What's the job?"

"Delivering a message."

"Where to?"

"Back at Wharf 62. Crate 6. But you've got to be quiet about it."

"On the q.t., eh? Well, Pem could give it a try. But he'd need to be paid in advance."

Randal was too weary to argue—and besides, he was sick of lugging the quarters around.

"What's the message?" Pembroke asked, slipping the coins into his bag.

"I'll tell you when we get there."

"Yer coming along? What's wrong, don't trust Pem?"

"Why should I?"

"Pem's as straight as Park Avenue."

Whether or not this was true, Randal conquered his exhaustion and led the way out of the forge. At the first bend in the pipe, he looked over his shoulder and saw that the pack rat had stopped some ways back, adding a paper clip to his bag.

"Come on, pack rat, we're in a hurry!"

"Sorry, yer honor. If it's a rush job, too, it'll be another dime."

Randal didn't have another dime. And so, to his intense annoyance, the pack rat stopped every time something shiny caught his eye. Which was at least once every couple of blocks. It was well after two a.m. before they reached the waterfront.

Everything was peaceful there. The West Side Highway had little traffic, and there wasn't a sound coming from Wharf 62.

"So, what's the message?" Pembroke asked.

"There'll be three rats asleep in crate 6," Randal said. "Two of them have rings on their tails. They'll probably be cuddled up together."

"I know them rings like the back of my paw," said Pembroke, who in a rare moment of sentimentality had slipped old Moony's ring onto Montague's tail. "What do you want me to tell 'em?"

"Don't wake them! The message is for the other one—the one without a ring. Tell her to bring her harmonica and meet me here. And tell her to be sure not to wake anybody else."

"Meet you here, eh? And what's yer honor's name?"

"Um, Gregory Sad-Rat."

"Sad-Rat? That's a new one."

"Just give her the message, pack rat. Then you can take your quarters and make yourself scarce."

Simple as the plan sounded, there was a hitch. The night dormouse. Normally, he would have been dozing on the job, but Maggie's jazzy music had stirred up his blood, and he still hadn't quite settled back down.

"And what would you be up to in the middle of the night, pack rat?" the little fellow asked, blocking the wharf's entrance crack.

"Delivery," Pembroke said.

"Delivery to what party?"

"Party in crate 6."

"You can leave it with me, whatever it is. I'll make sure they get it."

"Can't. Got to put it in their paws, personal. Orders."

"Then you'll have to come back in the morning. Everyone's sound asleep."

"Come on. Rats is mostly nocturnal."

"Not wharf rats. They never skulk around in the middle of the night. Unlike some."

Pembroke figured he could just brush the pint-sized mouse aside—but that wasn't the pack-rat way of doing things. He turned and crept back to the north side of the wharf, where Randal was peering down at the river. The beavers were chewing away at their fourth piling.

"No go, yer honor," Pembroke said.

"What do you mean, 'No go'?" Randal said, looking around at him.

"Won't let me in. Too late." Pembroke yawned. "If that's it, yer honor, I may go catch a few winks."

"What are you talking about? I paid you to do a job. It's not done."

"Well, if yer in the mood, you could take that key of yers and bop the dormouse on the head. While he's out, I'll take yer message."

Randal considered this. But while he was more than willing to destroy the entire wharf and send every rat he'd ever known plummeting into the Hudson River, he wasn't violent by nature.

"There must be a better way."

"You could always try a diversion, like Moony pulled in the art gallery."

"Diversion," Randal said thoughtfully. "That's not a bad idea. Don't dormice have a weakness for smelly cheeses?"

"It's common knowledge, yer honor."

"You wouldn't happen to have any smelly cheese in that sack of yours?"

"Sorry," Pembroke said—though in fact he did have a small hunk of Roquefort.

"Will you wait here while I get some?"

"When Pem signs on a job, he don't run out in the middle."

Randal wasn't wholly convinced. In fact, he thought of asking for his quarters back till the message was delivered. But then, the last thing a rat burglar needs is two quarters to carry around.

Robbing grocery stores is generally considered beneath the dignity of wharf rats. They leave that sort of thing to pack rats. But being out of funds, Randal had no choice—and at least he had an idea where to go. In his magazine hunts he'd often gotten a strong whiff of cheese when he passed a place called Ratner's Delicatessen.

At that hour, the deli was closed and dark, but Randal snuck in through the ventilation system and easily

sniffed his way to the cheese and dairy case. The case was chilly, but the assortment of cheeses was awe-inspiring, and it took Randal very little time to zero in on a particularly ripe piece of Limburger.

He lugged it back across the West Side Highway and dumped it on the curb. Then he crept back to the pack rat.

"Thanks for sticking around," Randal said.

"Limburger?" Pembroke asked, snout quivering.

"Mm-hm. Funny, though. I could swear I smell Roquefort over here."

"Snout must be playing tricks on you," said Pembroke, who had in fact just snacked on some.

"Look," Randal whispered as the night dormouse came sniffing his way out of the wharf's entrance crack. "Go on now, I'll watch your bag."

"That's okay, yer honor, I'm used to having it on my back."

When the dormouse was halfway to the Limburger, Pembroke hoisted his bag over his shoulder and tiptoed toward the entrance crack. As soon as he disappeared inside the wharf, Randal's eyes became as shifty as Pembroke's, flicking back and forth between the dormouse, gnawing cheese on the curb, and the beavers, gnawing on a piling down below.

The night dormouse had the worst table manners Randal had ever seen. The greedy little character got Limburger all over himself. By the time Maggie Mad-Rat followed the pack rat out of the wharf, the dormouse's entire head was buried in the chunk of cheese.

"Like I told you, Pem's good as his word," Pembroke said, leading Maggie over to Randal. "Anything else, yer honor?"

"No," said Randal. "But thanks, pack rat."

"Nice doing business with you."

Having squeezed the whole dollar out of this wharf rat, Pembroke figured their dealings were over, so he hitched up his bag and slipped away without saying any more about pipe whacking.

Maggie set down her harmonica and yawned. Yawns are infectious, and Randal was ordinarily a great yawner, but not now. One look at Maggie wiped away all his weariness. "Sorry to get you up so early, Maggie. But it's kind of an emergency."

"I hope you don't want any music," she said, rubbing the sleep out of her eyes. "I'm pretty played out."

"No, I just remembered you saying you were catching an early boat today . . ." Randal pointed across the West Side Highway. "Look, it's beginning to turn light in the east."

On the airplane Maggie hadn't minded yawning at the warthog's riddles, but she hated to yawn in Gregory's face. She couldn't help herself, though. For after the good-bye party was over, Isabel had kept her and Montague up telling them a story about Digby Dinner-Rat. The chef rat, it seemed, was the real firebug. He'd been trying to destroy Maggie's harmonica, not the crate, because he didn't like her music distracting people from his food. After much discussion Isabel and Montague had agreed that it would be heartless to get the poor old three-legged rat in trouble, but that in the morning they should drop the charges to keep the accused Randal Reese-Rat from being torn limb from limb. This settled, they'd all gone to bed. But that had been just a few minutes ago.

"What do you suppose that dormouse is up to, Gregory?" she asked, trying to disguise a yawn.

"Who knows?"

"So what's the emergency?"

Randal cleared his throat. "I was afraid I might

never see you again, and . . . it seemed like an emergency."

"Why, what a nice thing to say!" Even if he did blow hot and cold, there was something touching about this Gregory Sad-Rat. "I'm sorry, I really am pooped," she said as another yawn slipped out. "But you could always . . . my ship leaves at eight-thirty. The dock's not far—just up that way about a mile or so. If you'd like to see me off, you could meet me and my cousin and his wife there at around eight."

"But I was hoping to get to spend some time with you alone!"

He could always hop onboard the ship and come with her to see Africa. But Maggie realized that this was the sort of plan he would have to make on his own. "I'm afraid I really do have to get a little sleep. I'll look for you on the dock."

As she picked up her harmonica and turned to go back, Randal grabbed her tail.

"Hey!" she said, yanking it away.

"I'm sorry, but . . ."

"But what?"

"But . . . have you seen the Brooklyn Bridge yet?"

"The what?"

"The Brooklyn Bridge. You can't go back to Africa without seeing the Brooklyn Bridge! The reason I woke you so early is you have to cross downtown to get to it, and this is the only time of day downtown's not jammed with cars and people. If we hurry, we could watch the sun rise over the bridge. The arches are spectacular."

"Sounds like the one we crossed on our way in from the airport. It has a ratwalk above the traffic, right?"

Randal nodded glumly. The Brooklyn Bridge *did* have a raised ratwalk. As Maggie started toward the entrance crack once more, Randal again grabbed her tail in desperation.

"I'd heard New York rats have bad manners, but really!" she cried, jerking her tail free.

Maggie scurried back toward the entrance to the wharf with her harmonica, wondering at Gregory's odd behavior. At the zoo he'd barely bothered saying goodbye, and now he was tail grabbing! Yet just before reentering the wharf, she threw a glance over her shoulder—and she wasn't sorry to see the forlorn look on his face. He would, she thought, be on the dock at eight o'clock.

She was riding a zebra across the savanna in the moonlight, warm wind in her fur. Up ahead was a shimmering lake, but she knew that it was really just a vast puddle, no more than a few inches deep, and that the zebra could run right across it. But when they reached the edge, the zebra stopped short, throwing her off his back. She landed in something soft. Blinking, she saw that she was under a laurel bush, and that the big puddle was the reservoir in Central Park.

Maggie opened her eyes and saw that she was *really* in the new wing of crate 6 on Wharf 62. As she slipped off her cushion and crept toward the doorway, she heard Isabel's and Montague's voices just outside.

"Let her sleep, Monty. Then she'll miss her boat."

"But, Izzy, I think she really is homesick."

Maggie stepped out. "You're right, Monty," she said.

"I was just dreaming about Africa—sort of. What time is it?"

"Around seven-thirty," Isabel said. "Do you *have* to go?"

"I'm afraid so."

Isabel dashed over to crate 11 and returned with her parents and the bell her father used for calling emergency Grand Rat Chats. As soon as Isabel rang it, hundreds of sleepy rats came stumbling out of their crates, and Isabel climbed onto the little stage that had been erected for Maggie the night before.

"Sorry to wake you all," she cried, "but I was afraid some of you might go out on the rathunt again, and I wanted everyone to know that Monty and I are dropping the charges against Randal Reese-Rat. He didn't start the fire."

Mr. Reese-Rat had looked like a sleepwalker as he followed his wife and daughter out of crate 8, but now he was wide awake. "He didn't?" he said.

"No, he didn't," Isabel said firmly.

"Thank goodness!" cried Mrs. Reese-Rat.

"Who did then?" asked Bernie Bat-Rat.

Glancing over at crate 44, Isabel could see Digby Dinner-Rat propped in his doorway. "No one," she said. "It was an accident."

"But what about the charred matchsticks, Izzy?" said Mr. Moberly-Rat. "What about the evidence?"

"Yeah, what about that?" chimed one of Bernie's sidekicks.

"It was all a mistake," said Isabel. "Right, Monty?"

Montague climbed onto the stage beside her. "That's right, it was all a misunderstanding," he said. "So now everyone can go back to bed."

"But first say good-bye to Maggie," said Isabel. "She's taking off for Africa."

Some of the rats started whispering among themselves, but most waved to Maggie.

"Bye, Maggie!"

"Come back soon!"

"Yeah, and bring your harmonica!"

Maggie waved as she walked to the entrance of the wharf, followed by Isabel and Montague and Mr. and Mrs. Moberly-Rat. The dormouse jumped to attention as the august group passed by.

"I must say, Izzy, I think it's very odd, simply dropping the charges like that," Mr. Moberly-Rat said, stopping just outside the wharf. "Most irregular. Don't you agree, Lavinia?"

"Daddy, we're saying good-bye to Maggie," Isabel said, "not holding court."

"Oh, indeed, quite right, my dear. We wish you'd stay, Maggie. We've hardly had a chance to get to know you."

"Promise you won't be a stranger, dear," Mrs. Moberly-Rat said, giving Maggie a kiss on the snout.

As Maggie thanked them for putting her up, Montague took the harmonica off her paws, then the three young rats headed up the edge of the West Side Highway. Mr. Moberly-Rat's tail twitched away as he waved, but the only part of Mrs. Moberly-Rat that twitched was her snout.

"Where on earth did you get Limburger, dormouse?" she asked sharply.

"I didn't, ma'am," said the dormouse, standing straight as a poker. "But the night mouse—Lord, you should have seen him. He was so stuffed he'd passed out. I had to drag him home."

"And where did *he* get his paws on Limburger?"

"I've no idea, ma'am."

"I haven't had any Limburger in ages, Hugh."

"Are you sure, Lavinia?" Mr. Moberly-Rat said. "Are you quite certain? I could have sworn I saw you with a piece of Limburger just last Tuesday. Or was it Monday?"

While they debated the cheese issue, Maggie and Isabel and Montague made their way northward to the dock from which ships departed for Africa. The ship moored there, the SS *MauRatania*, wasn't anywhere near the size of the cruise ship Maggie's mother had taken to the Caribbean.

"That settles it, you have to stay," Isabel declared. "If there's a storm at sea, that thing would go down like a pack rat diving for a dime."

"Oh, I'm sure she's seaworthy," Maggie said.

"You really think so? I don't even see how you'll get onboard."

Human beings were using a crane to load boxes of

electronic goods onto the foredeck, but the gangplank had already been raised.

"Mother sometimes uses the stern line," Maggie said, pointing at a rope stretching from a cleat on the dock up to the ship's rear deck.

"With your harmonica?" Isabel said. "You'll fall!"

"No, I won't. I don't want to boast, but I once tightrope-walked a vine over a river full of tiger fish. The trick is not to look down."

"What are tiger fish?"

"They live in African rivers. They're ugly as sin—and carnivorous."

"Carnivorous?"

"Rat-eating."

"Gad!"

Maggie relieved her cousin of her harmonica. "Thanks, Monty. I'm really glad I got to be at your wedding."

"Us, too," said Montague. "Without you the reception would have been a big dud."

Maggie scanned the dock. Except for a few longshoremen, and a dirty-looking seagull perched atop a piling, it was pretty much deserted. Not a sign of Gregory Sad-Rat. She hesitated a moment, feeling strangely disappointed, then kissed Montague and Isabel good-bye. "If you visit my father's grave, tell him I'm thinking of him."

"We will," said the newlyweds.

Using her African-vine technique of not looking

down, Maggie negotiated the stern line successfully. She stepped onto the ship's rear deck—and a massive sailor with a thick black beard let out a shriek and ran for his life.

Maggie leaned her harmonica against a coil of rope and looked back down at the dock. Monty and Isabel were perched by the cleat waving up at her, their tails entwined.

Suddenly, there was a loud groan. The crane ground to a halt. A box dangling in a net swayed back and forth in midair. The crane operator cursed loudly, as did the longshoremen.

A delay, it looked like. Maggie thought of hiding her harmonica and tightroping back to the dock to pass the time with Isabel and Montague. But when she looked down in their direction, she saw that they'd already left.

I guess they were in too much of a hurry to wait and see me off, Maggie thought with a prick of sadness.

And Gregory hadn't come at all.

Isabel and Montague had intended to see the boat off, but at the very same moment the crane stopped, Isabel caught sight of Bernie Bat-Rat and his gang racing up the other side of the West Side Highway.

"What do you think they're up to?" she said.

"Hunting for money?" Montague suggested.

"Doesn't look that way. We better check."

But when they reached the curb of the West Side Highway, they were greeted by a thick stream of cars and trucks. A light must have changed. By the time there was a break in the traffic, the gang had vanished.

"We should head back to the wharf," said Isabel. "Maybe Daddy'll know what they're doing."

They hustled down to Wharf 62, where they found Isabel's father talking to Mr. Reese-Rat in front of crate 8.

"Back already, Izzy?" said Mr. Moberly-Rat. "That was quick."

"There was a posse heading uptown, Daddy. I didn't like the look of it."

"A bunch of young hotheads," Mr. Moberly-Rat said. "Whippersnappers who won't listen to their elders."

"Are they looking for Randal?"

"I tried to stop them, sweetheart. And Clarence revoked his reward. But they're not out for money, they're out for blood. They think you're covering for your old friend, the hooligans!"

"Now, Isabel, you must tell me," said Mr. Reese-Rat. "Are you dropping the charges out of sentiment, or are you really sure of Randal's innocence?"

"He didn't do it, Mr. Reese-Rat."

"Who did then?"

Since Randal's life seemed to be in real danger, Isabel figured she'd better tell the two rat leaders what she'd found out about Digby Dinner-Rat. "But we don't want to press charges against Digby," she said. "He didn't mean to set the crate on fire, just the harmonica."

"I knew it!" Mr. Reese-Rat cried. "I knew no son of mine could be a firebug."

"We have to find Randal before that gang of goons does," said Isabel. "He could never hold his own against them."

"Are you saying my son's not a fighter?"

In fact, Isabel *didn't* think of Randal as much of a fighter, what with his toothbrush and his cologne. But she was too diplomatic to say this. "I meant, since he was poisoned so recently, he won't be up to snuff."

"Ah, yes." Mr. Reese-Rat scratched his head. "But if he didn't start the fire, why do you suppose he disappeared in the middle of the night like that?"

"Well, Mr. Reese-Rat, I've been thinking. Maybe he just didn't like the idea of living next door to Monty and me."

"Hm," said Mr. Reese-Rat. "I guess I could understand that. But where would he have gone?"

"Maybe somewhere underground."

"Reese-Rats don't go underground!"

"Perhaps you should organize a search party, Clarence," said Mr. Moberly-Rat.

This was exactly what Mr. Reese-Rat did. But since he instructed the rats to look in the streets and parks, Isabel, who was beginning to feel partly responsible for Randal's woes, convinced Montague to help her conduct a subterranean search.

Familiar as Montague was with the city's underground network, an hour of ransacking the storm sewers and drainage pipes turned up only a few brown rats, none of whom had seen anyone with a Band-Aid on his tail or a key around his neck. When the searchers happened to pass near the Mad-Rats' home, Isabel decided they should check there, and though Montague was doubtful, knowing how little besides hats and mud castles registered on his parents, the first thing Isabel saw when they turned down the sewer pipe was a toothbrush.

"This is Randal's, I'd know it anywhere!" she cried. "Maybe your family's putting him up."

The Mad-Rats were not putting Randal up. But when they described him to Mrs. Mad-Rat, she told them he'd been there last night looking for Maggie.

"Maggie?" said Isabel.

"That's what he said, dearie."

Isabel and Montague blinked at each other through the smoke.

"What was the name of that rat Maggie met at the zoo?" Montague murmured.

"Sad-Rat," said Isabel. "Gregory Sad-Rat."

"Funny name, huh?" said Montague.

"Mm. And Randal's grandfather's name was Gregory."

"Did you tell him where Maggie was, Mom?"

"I only told him what I knew," said Mrs. Mad-Rat.

"That Maggie was spending the night over on that wharf. Um, you know, Monty, I was wondering . . ."

But before she could drop a hint about her supplies, Montague and Isabel were dashing away, heading back to the wharf.

When Maggie left Randal crouching alone outside the wharf, Randal fell into a ratatonic state, staring out blankly at the moony river while the night dormouse ate himself into a Limburger cheese stupor. Losing Isabel to Montague the upstart had been terrible, but this was infinitely worse. That had made him angry and indignant. Maggie's desertion left him feeling as empty and shattered as one of the broken dandelion-wine bottles he'd swept out of his hideout.

After a while he crept along the edge of Wharf 62 till he was right above where the beavers were at work. Amazingly, they'd already gnawed through half the pilings. He shinnied down to the cross brace they were standing on.

"Rat!" said Bobo, looking around in surprise. "What are you doing down here?"

"I wanted to let you know you could take a break."

"But we're half done," said Bobo, spitting wood chips into the stagnant river water. "If we keep at it, we'll—"

"The thing is," Randal said, "I'd rather you finished later in the day. Would you mind terribly?" Even though Maggie had turned her back on him, he couldn't bear to think of her tumbling into the Hudson River.

"We could use a rest," Buck panted. "It's pretty rugged work."

"But at least it's not slave labor, Buck," said Bobo. "We're free. And we have each other."

They had each other, Randal thought with a silent sigh.

While resting, the beavers started quietly discussing their plans. Once they finished off the pilings, they would swim straight upriver to find a new home. They would construct a new dam, and a new lodge, complete with a private swimming pool, where they would be able to teach their future children how to dive and fish.

Randal stared down morosely at the stagnant water. The beavers were talking about building a new home—and what was he doing? Destroying the homes of his family and every wharf rat he'd ever known. And why? To pay them back for unjustly condemning him. But what would be so bad about getting caught and being hung from the wharf rafters? It seemed odd, but now that he'd lost Maggie Mad-Rat—found and lost

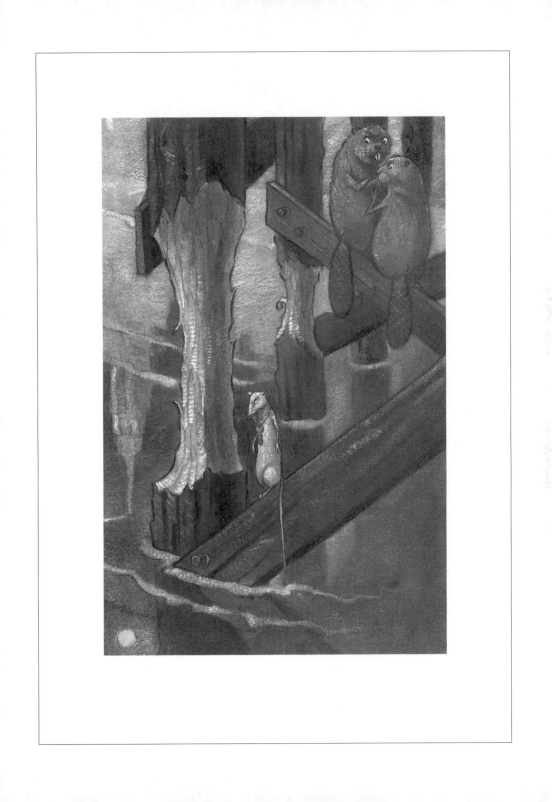

her all in one day—he no longer really cared what happened to him. Where would he ever find another rat who suited him as she did? Nowhere. So what was the point of going on?

Soon a pearly glaze of daylight seeped over the river, by which time the beavers had dozed off, one propping up the other. Then, as the sun rose over the skyscrapers, the river took on a golden sheen, like the savanna in Randal's zebra photo. Even the dirty waters beneath the wharf brightened. But not Randal's mood. Isabel and her Mad-Rat groom would be seeing Maggie off for Africa. And Randal would never set eyes on her again.

He gave Bobo a nudge.

"Gosh, I was dreaming we were putting the finishing touches on our new dam," Bobo said, blinking.

"Funny, so was I," said Buck.

"Go ahead," said Randal.

"What do you mean?" said Buck.

"Go build your dam. You should just about have time to finish one before winter comes."

"You don't want us to finish the pilings for you?" said Buck.

"Nah, it doesn't seem worth the effort," said Randal. "But thanks anyway."

"You sound blue, rat," Buck said.

"What's the matter?" said Bobo.

"Nothing. I'm just feeling sorry for myself. But that's not your problem. You guys can take off."

"But we don't want to leave you feeling down," Bobo said. "You're our savior—our champion."

"Ever since those little tranquilizer bullets got under our pelts," said Buck, "I figured the old saying about good things coming in small packages was all wrong. But you've proven it's right, rat. You may be small, but you're just about the biggest thing that ever happened to us."

"Thanks," Randal said with a sigh.

"What's your name, anyway?" Bobo asked.

"Randal. Randal Reese-Rat."

"You know what, Buck?"

"What?"

"I think I know the name of our first male child."

"Excellent idea. Has a nice ring to it—Randal."

"Randal!"

Randal nearly fell backward off the cross brace. That last "Randal" had come not from the beavers but from somewhere up above.

"Randal!" came the cry again. "It's Izzy! Are you around here anywhere?"

"Sounds like a she-rat," Bobo said encouragingly.

"Randal Reese-Rat!" came Isabel's voice again. "Please answer if you can hear me! We know you didn't start the fire!"

Randal didn't say a word.

"Gregory!" the voice cried. "Gregory Sad-Rat! Please answer if you can hear me! We know you're innocent!"

This electrified Randal. Not because Isabel knew he was innocent but because she knew his fake name. There was only one rat who could have told her that. And if that rat had mentioned him, it seemed possible—just possible—that that rat didn't think he was a total zero.

"Excuse me a minute, will you?" Randal said.

"Of course," Bobo and Buck said in unison.

Randal clawed his way up the piling and crawled along the edge of the wharf. When he stepped ashore, there stood Isabel, with her new husband at her side.

"Randal!" she cried. "I'm so glad to see you!"

Randal just grunted, not really knowing what to say to her.

"Where in the world have you been?"

"Oh, here and there."

"But . . . did you know about the fire?"

"I heard about it."

"Did you know everyone thought you set it?"

"I heard that, too."

"We know you didn't."

"Well, that's good."

"But Bernie and some of his pals are out looking for you. We're afraid they might string you up or something."

Randal shrugged.

"I don't think we've met," Montague said. "I'm Montague Mad-Rat."

Montague stuck out his paw. After a moment's hesi-

tation, Randal shook it. "Randal Reese-Rat," he mumbled.

"Nice to meet you. I think you met my cousin, Maggie?"

"Um, yesterday. At the zoo."

"Pretty, isn't she?"

"Mm."

Montague sensed, correctly, that Randal wasn't very comfortable with him there, so he drifted several paces away and turned to the river. Out in the middle, the tides created good-sized waves, and the way the sun flashed and flickered off them made his paws itch to paint. He'd never used the river for a subject.

"What a coincidence, you and Maggie running into each other," Isabel said to Randal. "Isn't she the best?"

"She seems very nice," Randal said.

"I think she likes you."

"Really?"

"Well, if you go by Gregory Sad-Rat, she does."

"Did you see her boat off?"

"Uh-huh."

"So she's left for Africa."

"Actually, I think her boat may have been delayed. Loading problems."

"You mean, it might still be at the dock?"

"It might."

But just as Randal felt his spirits rising, they got shot down—by Montague, as usual.

"I hate to say it," Montague said, pointing out at a couple of ships heading downriver, "but I think one of those is Maggie's."

While the human beings were fixing the crane, Maggie watched from the *MauRatania*'s rear deck. Isabel and Montague never came back, and Gregory Sad-Rat never showed up at all. In fact, the only rat she spotted on the dock was a pack rat who grabbed a shiny screw that had fallen out of the crane and stuck it into his bag. She wasn't absolutely positive, but she thought it was the same pack rat who'd woken her up before dawn.

Finally, the crane started working again, and the last boxes were loaded. An air horn tooted from the ship's bridge. Down below on the dock, men pulled the stern and aft lines from their cleats, and the ship steamed away.

This was Maggie's first time on a North American river. There was no peanut gallery of monkeys making sarcastic comments from the banks. There were no hippos or water buffalo cooling off in the current. There were no vines and no tiger fish—at least none that you could make out. But, funnily enough, as the ship arched to the south, Maggie wasn't thinking of her beloved African rivers. She was thinking of Isabel—Isabel as she'd last seen her, with her tail twined around Montague's. How nice it must be to have someone to share things with, as Isabel did! Cheese, riddles, a nest at night.

The big, bearded sailor had never returned, so Maggie pattered right across the rear deck to the port side. The ship was bucking the tide, but the dock was already a ways behind them. Up ahead, she could make out Wharf 62. Much farther ahead, just visible in the hazy sunlight, a spectacular suspension bridge spanned the mouth of the harbor. She was pretty sure it wasn't the Brooklyn Bridge, but still it made her think of Gregory Sad-Rat. The memory of the encounter with him outside the wharf seemed as strange and dreamlike as the zebra ride. How odd his sending that pack rat to wake her up so early. And then grabbing her tail!

But other than that, Gregory certainly hadn't been impolite. And looked at from a certain angle, the tail grabbing was kind of flattering, a sign of how eager he'd been to show her that Brooklyn Bridge. Maybe she shouldn't have been so concerned about her sleep. By ship the trip was going to take a week, and she could loll around the whole time if she wanted.

She pattered back to the starboard side and saw a truly ghoulish sight: a statue of a gigantic green human-female firebug. It really would be a relief to get back to Africa, where human beings weren't everywhere you looked.

Still, she couldn't help feeling she was leaving something of herself behind in the overcrowded city. Perhaps it had to do with her father. It had been an emotional experience, spending the night on his grave. And then, too, she'd grown awfully fond of Montague and Isabel, and of her eccentric aunt and uncle as well.

Yet it was more than that. She picked up her harmonica and played a few bars, then set it down and
sang the city a farewell song.

> *New York City scary,*
> *Subway make you shiver,*
> *Fire start in rat wharf,*
> *On the Hudson River.*
>
> *But wharf rat fan of music,*
> *Generous applause;*
> *After every number,*
> *Many clapping paws.*
>
> *Bye to fun with Izzy*
> *And Cousin Montague,*
> *Bye to fun in sewer*
> *And also in the—*

Maggie stopped abruptly as a rat heaved himself over the ship's gunwale and collapsed in a heap at her feet. It was a he-rat with a key around his neck.

"Gregory?" Maggie said, wondering if she was dreaming again. "Is that you?"

The rat was gasping too much to speak, but he lifted his head from the deck and nodded.

"Is that *really* you?"

The rat gave another gasping nod.

"Are you all right?"

He scraped himself off the deck and leaned back against the coil of rope. He looked like a drowned rat. His fur was soaked and every which way, and instead of a neat Band-Aid on his tail, there was a greenish splotch.

"I never thought I'd make it, Maggie," he said, running a paw across his face. "Halfway up I was sure I was a goner."

"But—but where did you come from?"

"I shinnied up that rope."

Maggie peered over the gunwale. Since the big, bearded sailor had never returned to pull up the stern line, it was trailing behind in the ship's wake.

"You were swimming in the river?" she said, more amazed by the moment.

"Not exactly."

"Then how did you get to that rope?"

"It's a long story."

"Well, we have plenty of time—unless you plan to jump ship before we get out of the harbor. Did you know I'd be onboard?"

"Well, I, um, I hoped you would. There's another ship behind you, the HMS *Rattigan*. But I figured it was this one."

"Why?"

"This one's the *MauRatania*."

"How do you know about *MauRatania*?"

"From a vervet monkey at the zoo. It's the country next door to Senegal, right?"

"You really know your Africa! And you must be an awfully strong swimmer, too."

"Well, I had help."

"From?"

"Well, Izzy, for starters. And Montague."

"Really! I had no idea you knew them. Aren't they wonderful?"

"Well . . . they're not bad."

"I didn't know they were such good swimmers."

"No, the beavers swam me out."

"Beavers? What're they?"

"North American mammals. They're masterful in the water."

"But what about Monty and Izzy?"

He didn't want to tell her what Isabel had said about her liking him, because he still wasn't sure she really did like him. "Well, I didn't think I could just skip town," he said. "You see, I had an obligation to a chimpanzee at the zoo. I'd promised to get him a banana every day for a month. But Montague said he'd take care of it for me. That freed me up to go."

"Have you always wanted to visit Africa?"

"Actually, I've never really thought about it."

"Then why did you come aboard?"

Randal stood up. He could see what a mess he was, but he didn't mind. The last few hours had changed him. He didn't care if he never saw another toothbrush or bottle of cologne again.

"It was because of you," he said.

"Really?"

"I know I don't look like much, Maggie—especially at the moment. But even so, I hope you'll at least *think* about marrying me."

"Why, how funny!"

"Funny?" he said, taken aback.

"Funny strange, I mean. I was just thinking how nice it would be to have someone to share things with—then up you pop, out of nowhere!"

Randal grinned. The sun was starting to dry his fur, and now its warmth began to penetrate inside him.

"So you really will think about it?"

"No."

"You won't?" he said, crestfallen.

"I don't need to think about it."

"You don't?"

She gave him a kiss on the snout. "No."

"You mean you accept!"

Maggie nodded.

"Hooray!" he cried. "We'll live together in Africa!"

So much for all his photos. Now he would get to see the real thing! For the first time in his life, he broke into song:

Up the river Niger,
Water buffalo
Not the only creature
Making progress slow.

For the second verse, Maggie accompanied him on harmonica.

Up the river Niger,
What a lot of fuss

When the water full of
Hippopotamus.

"I can't wait!" Randal cried. "It'll be so much fun! I wish we could get married right now!"

"Well, I hope we can wait till December."

"December?"

"That's when Mother's coming for a visit. I am her only child, and she wouldn't want to miss it."

That meant they wouldn't be able to cuddle for three months. But still, they could talk, and do things together. "Whatever you say, Maggie."

"Oh, and one other little thing."

"What?"

"Well, Gregory, it's your last name. I really don't think I could be Maggie Sad-Rat. I'm almost never sad. So, if you don't mind, could you take my name instead?"

Randal's jaw dropped, hitting his key. "Mad-Rat?"

"Would that be all right?"

She wanted him, Randal Reese-Rat, to be a Mad-Rat? To share a name with the upstart and his nutcase family? If his grandfather hadn't been dead already, the idea of a grandson of his turning into a Mad-Rat would have surely done him in.

But then, his grandfather *had* already crossed the gulf to the land of dead rats. And so had Randal Reese-Rat, with his grooming and yawning. And so, for that matter, had Gregory Sad-Rat, with his sighing and moping.

"Mad-Rat's okay by me," he said.

"Oh, good!"

He glanced over his shoulder. "Listen, I'm sorry about my tail. It got poisoned. I hope you don't mind."

"Oh, but war wounds are nice," Maggie said—proving that Ellie wasn't as knuckleheaded as he thought.

He moved over beside Maggie and twined his tail with hers. Even though he was turning himself into a Mad-Rat, he'd never been so happy in his life.

"Don't you wish they could all come for the wedding?" Maggie murmured, leaning her head on his shoulder.

"Who?"

"All of them," she said, pointing.

He just smiled. There, in the hazy distance, growing smaller by the second, was Wharf 62. Half its pilings were weakened, but, thanks to him, the rest would stand firm. After he'd shinnied a few feet up the *Mau-Ratania*'s stern line, the beavers had thumped their flat tails in farewell and shouted up a final offer to finish off the pilings for him—but he'd shouted down: "Save your teeth for your dam, beavers!"

Thinking of that, he could all but hear Mr. Hugh Moberly-Rat's fine, screechy voice: "We are gathered here today to celebrate the marriage of Maggie Mad-Rat to the young rat responsible for the very fact that we are . . . gathered here today."

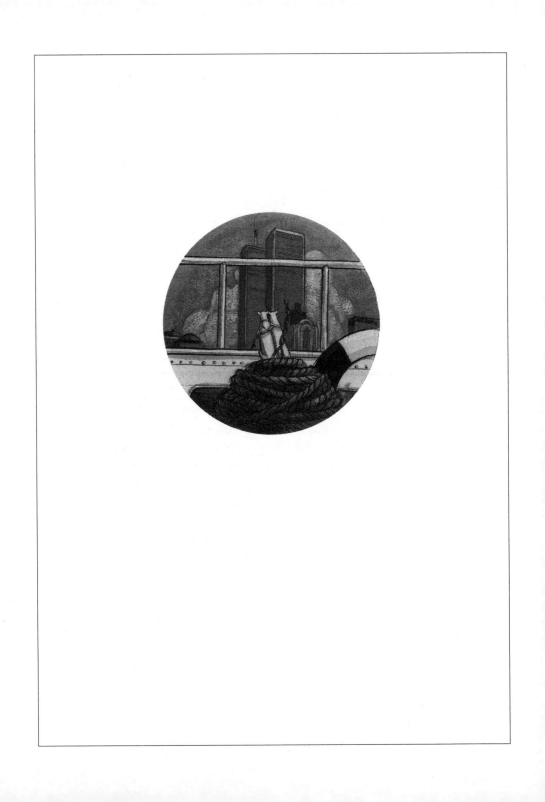